Anna's

Amish Fears Revealed

THE AMISH WOMEN OF
LAWRENCE COUNTY SERIES - BOOK 3

Tracy Fredrychowski

ISBN 978-1-7371172-8-5 (paperback)

ISBN 978-1-7371172-7-8 (digital)

All Bible verses are taken from King James Version (KJV)

Published in South Carolina by The Tracer Group, LLC

https://tracyfredrychowski.com

i

"What time I am afraid, I will trust in thee."

Psalm 56:3 (KJV)

By Tracy Fredrychowski

AMISH OF LAWRENCE COUNTY SERIES
Secrets of Willow Springs – Book 1
Secrets of Willow Springs – Book 2
Secrets of Willow Springs – Book 3

APPLE BLOSSOM INN SERIES
Love Blooms at the Apple Blossom Inn
An Amish Christmas at the Apple Blossom Inn

NOVELLA'S
The Amish Women of Lawrence County
An Amish Gift Worth Waiting For

THE AMISH WOMEN OF LAWRENCE COUNTY
Emma's Amish Faith Tested – Book 1
Rebecca's Amish Heart Restored – Book 2
Anna's Amish Fears Revealed – Book 3

www.tracyfredrychowski.com

Tracy Fredrychowski

Contents

ABOUT THIS STORY...

While this story and its characters are figments of my imagination, Jesus Christ is very much the truth.

Throughout the United States and Canada, there are some conservative Amish orders that practice salvation through works. They believe only God can decide their eternal destiny by how well they stayed in obedience to the rules of the *Ordnung.*

Many Amish communities share traditional beliefs, much like today's Christians. However, some think the assurance of eternal salvation to be prideful and refuse to accept the truth as written in God's Word.

As I researched this story, I found more Amish communities are moving away from their old ways. It was heart-warming to discover the truth was being taught, and they have assurance in salvation through Jesus Christ alone.

Please keep in mind not all Amish Orders are the same. And while I write the truth about finding salvation in Christ, what is practiced among the Amish may differ from community to community across the country.

A NOTE ABOUT AMISH VOCABULARY

The Amish language is called Pennsylvania Dutch and is usually spoken rather than written. The spelling of commonly used words varies from community to community throughout the United States and Canada. Even as I researched this book, some words' spelling changed within the same Amish community that inspired this story. In one case, spellings were debated between family members. Some of the terms may have slightly different spellings. Still, all come from my interactions with the Amish settlement near where I was raised in northwestern Pennsylvania.

While this book was modeled upon a small community in Lawrence County, this is a work of fiction. The names and characters are products of my imagination. They do not resemble any person, living or dead, or actual events in that community.

LIST OF CHARACTERS

Anna Byler. Fearful and hurt twenty-five-year-old Amish woman.

Simon Kaufmann. Former fiancé' to Anna, who has returned to Willow Springs hoping to rekindle their relationship.

Jebediah & Naomi Kaufmann. Simon's mother and father.

Neal & Margaret Buckhannon. Steven's maternal grandparents.

Rebecca Bricker. Anna's twin sister and wife to Eli.

Emma Yoder. Rebecca and Anna's younger sister and wife to Samuel.

Ruth Yoder. Matthew, Anna, Rebecca, and Emma's deceased mother's best friend and mother to Katie.

Jacob & Wilma Byler. Matthew, Anna, Rebecca, and Emma's father and stepmother.

MAP OF WILLOW SPRINGS

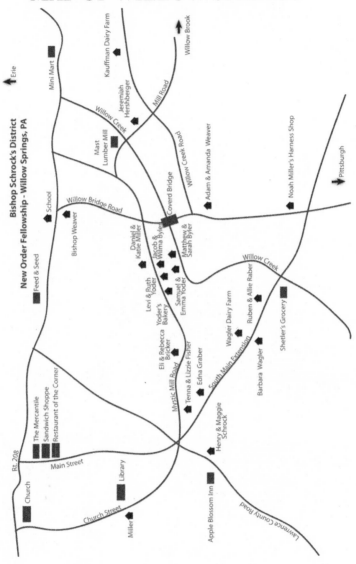

PROLOGUE – BOOK 3

September - Willow Springs, Pennsylvania

A heaviness pressed down on Anna Byler's chest, and she reached out to catch herself from falling. Her heart raced in anticipation all morning of having to go to Shetler's Grocery. Her *schwester*, Rebecca, continued to push her out of the house. But in all reality, she felt the safest tending to the chickens or helping with chores.

The grocery shelf shook under her weight. Before she had a chance to slip to the floor gracefully, her arm caught a stack of cans, making a commotion clamored throughout the store.

A fuzziness floated before her eyes, and she squeezed them tight, praying it would pass quickly. An awful buzz echoed in her ears, and she leaned forward to put her head between her knees and prayed. *Please, Lord, make it go away.*

A tender voice and a warm hand on her back made her tip her head toward the calming call.

"What is it, Anna? Are you ill?"

Even if she wanted to answer Naomi Kauffman, she couldn't form two audible words. The old woman called out. "Simon, where are you?"

Did she hear correctly? Had Naomi called for Simon? *Oh, please, Lord, not Simon. He can't see me like this.*

She tried to stand up with a shuddering sigh, only to fall to her knees.

Mrs. Kauffman supported her arm. "No child, stay put. Simon is here. Let him help you."

The aroma of pine shavings and diesel fuel swirled under her nose, revealing Simon's closeness. After all their years apart, his job at Mast Lumber Mill did little but remind her of the plans they once had.

Their paths rarely crossed since he'd returned to Willow Springs. When he followed his dream instead of his heart three years ago, she'd all but written that part of her life off. But his touch only added to the panic creeping through her skin.

Anguish filled her until the weight crushed her lungs, preventing her from taking an easy breath. Try as she might, she pulled her arm from his grip, but it only caused her knees to buckle further. Simon placed his arms under her legs and around her waist and picked her up quickly.

The sudden rush forced her head to drop into his chest. She stopped fighting and let his strong arms cradle her body without any option but to allow him to carry her.

"Relax, Anna, I've got you."

She didn't have the strength to argue and thought, *Relax? How dare he think I can relax in his arms after all he's done?*

Simon stopped near the cash register and put Anna in the chair Mr. Shetler had pulled out. Simon snapped his head toward the direction of the people who had hovered around them. "Someone! A glass of water."

Simon fell to one knee, rested his hand under her arm, and leaned closer. "Did you have another panic attack?"

There weren't many people outside her immediate family who knew she suffered from spells of anxiety. She'd hoped to keep it that way. When she lifted her face toward the crowd, her heart sank. She leaned onto Simon's shoulder and begged, "Please make them go away."

Simon stood and guided her toward the door. "She's fine. Just a little overheated. A glass of water and she'll be good as new."

Naomi followed them outside and opened the passenger side door of Simon's truck. After helping Anna to the leather seat, he thanked his mother.

Mrs. Kauffman leaned inside and handed Anna a cup of water. "Here, dear, drink this and let Simon turn on the air conditioner to cool you down."

Naomi let her hand come to rest on her son's forearm. "I won't be but a few more minutes. Perhaps we should take her home?"

Tears blurred Anna's vision. "I've made a scene. I'm so sorry."

The older woman patted her arm. "Now, don't think another thing of it. These things happen."

Anna looked worried. "Naomi, if the *People* catch you speaking to me, you'll get in trouble. You know I'm shunned, and you're not allowed to talk to me."

Mrs. Kauffman's tender tone calmed her fears. "You let me worry about that. No one will tell me I can't help someone who needs assistance. It will take more than this to ruffle my feathers."

Simon shut the door and Anna closed her eyes against the sudden tears, leaned her head back on the seat and thought, *Why does this continue to happen to me? And of all people, why did it have to be Simon?* That part of her heart had long closed, and every time she was around him, all it did was stir up memories she had tried to bury.

She opened her eyes when Simon slid into the driver's seat. If fear alone didn't paralyze her, the picture hanging from his rearview mirror and the fishing lure she'd bought him made her gasp for air.

Bile settled in the back of her throat, forcing her to flee the truck. The hue of color from the changing seasons gave her no comfort as she ran across the road and through the field that led back to her *schwester* Rebecca's house. Even the pounding of her heart couldn't block out his cry.

"Anna…please! Let me explain."

CHAPTER 1

Anna fell to her knees, pulse thrashing in her chest. Simon's voice long faded, but his eyes the color of the pebbles along Willow Creek, and his dark turned-up curls beneath his baseball cap were stamped behind her eyelids.

Kneeling at the foot of her mother's grave, she cried. "Oh *Mamm*, how will I ever get over Simon? Ever since he returned to Willow Springs, my heart is all twisted, and all I want to do is run away. But where would I go? *Datt* has disowned me since I decided to leave the church and join the New Order Fellowship, and all I have left of you is this place you share with hundreds of wooden crosses. I feel so lost and alone. Why did you have to go so soon?

I've spent time reading my Bible like our new bishop, Henry Schrock, suggested, but I'm still paralyzed by fear. I'm comforted by the Word, but I'm having trouble applying it to my life. How can Jesus, who knows all my thoughts, deliver me from this constant dread? It's like a chain around my heart, with no key to set me free. When I asked Bishop Schrock, he said, *"Christ holds the key, and he can unlock and banish you from all your fears if you lay them down at his feet."*

I try *Mamm*, really, I do, but whenever I think I've finally rid myself of worry and fear and hand it over to Him in my heart, something happens. I go and pick up the same concern all over again. How can I say I'm a Christian if I keep reverting to my old ways? Oh, *Mamm*, will God ever forgive me of unfaithfulness?

There are days I'm not even sure what I'm fearful about. But I know since Simon's return, the fear of allowing my heart to be broken again is stronger than ever. I've lost so many things in the last few years that I'm always anticipating the next trial.

First your death, then *Datt's* refusal to accept my choice to follow Jesus, and Simon's broken promises. How will I ever trust again? When I gave myself to Jesus, I thought all my worries would disappear. That somehow, His voice would be stronger, and I'd overcome the hold anxiety has on me. I've learned God has worked powerfully in people's lives throughout the ages. Why isn't he doing the same for me?

Mamm, how often do I come to your gravesite and pour out my cares? It's the one place in all of Willow Springs I feel you, even though I know nothing is left of you here but a distant memory.

The panic attacks are coming on stronger these days. Before, I could take a few deep breaths and stop them, but now they have taken control of my life. I agonize over them daily. My heart beats so loud I swear it will explode without warning, and my breath escapes, leaving me so weak I can barely stand. It's terrifying, especially when it happens in public, like today at Shetler's.

I've done everything I can think of to stop them. I spend time praying, asking God to help me, not thinking about them. But I don't know what triggers an episode. I'd surely find a way to avoid those situations if I did. I've even written my worries down and burned them, but nothing. They suffocate me to the point I'm finding it hard to leave the house.

Church is about all I can handle these days, and that is getting more challenging since Simon has taken to attending.

This past Sunday, Samuel preached how God solicited Moses to deliver His people. Moses argued with God, telling him he wasn't equipped to carry out His plan to meet with Pharaoh. That's how I feel. I'm not worthy to carry out God's plans. I promise to stop worrying, but I fail repeatedly. How can God trust me with His promises if I can't keep mine?

Oh, *Mamm*, why did Simon come back after all these years? Can't he see his presence upsets me? Leaving the Amish to follow his dream is one thing but breaking his promises to me is another. I see how he looks at me.

I want to trust again. But what happens if…I'm not strong enough to go through that again, especially after all he's done? God may have forgiven him, but can I?"

A flock of birds perched high in a maple tree averted Anna's attention away from her one-sided conversation with her deceased mother. She pulled herself to her feet and brushed the crushed crimson leaves from her wool stockings.

In the quiet of the cool September morning, Anna stared at the host of sparrows finding shelter in the fall foliage. Minister Samuel Yoder's message from Sunday played over in her head.

We're doomed to fail when we try to convince ourselves that we know more than God. God's plan doesn't include us growing in our own self-confidence. He wants us to put all our trust in Him. After all, isn't it only God who is powerful enough to overcome all the pharaohs in our lives?

Anna shielded her eyes and tried to focus on the flight of birds through the sunshine filtering on her face and thought, *I'm nowhere as faithful as Moses. I certainly can't do all you ask of me. Why can't I just be like the birds in the sky and not have a care in the world?*

With a shuddering sigh, she mumbled, "I best go face Rebecca and tell her I can't even be trusted to pick up a few groceries without crumbling to pieces."

***

Simon followed the sway of Anna's green dress as she ran across the road and into the field, running perpendicular to South Main Street Extension. All the families living on Mystic Mill Road used the well-worn shortcut.

It was high time Anna stopped ignoring him and let him clarify his return. Everyone, including his own family, welcomed him home. But the one person who had a pull on his heart greater than anyone else in Willow Springs turned gray every time she saw him.

There was so much riding on his ability to win Anna back that there was little else he could concentrate on. Even his part-time job at Mast Lumber Mill did little to divert his attention from the one woman who held him captive.

He would have chased her down if it weren't for his mother's voice. "Where's Anna?"

Simon moved around the truck and placed his mother's groceries in the back seat. "She decided to walk home."

"Walk? She could barely stand a few minutes ago. I can't believe you didn't stop her."

Simon let his mother rattle on while stacking the bags of bulk food items neatly on the bench seat.

"Mr. Shetler charged Anna's items to Eli and Rebecca's account and inquired if we could drop them off on our way home."

The box contained an array of pantry items, but the jar of Karo syrup and bag of Spanish peanuts caught his eye. The two generic items brought back a muckle of memories, so fresh that his mouth watered at the mere thought of Anna's famous peanut brittle. On more than one occasion, he thought of asking his mother to make it, but it wouldn't be the same if he enjoyed it on his own. Instead, he often stopped at Yoder's Bakery, knowing Anna sold it there.

For two years, as they planned and plotted their life together, a jar of the crunchy candy always made its way to the top of his tackle box. As the creek bubbled over the rocks, he fell in love with Anna Byler. Her chestnut hair and hazel-gray eyes lured him as much as the fluke bait he used to entice the fish in the creek.

But much like the taste of the salty-sweet brittle, their love faded as he picked the world over her. For years he hid his pain in the glory of prestige, traveling the country fishing professionally. His dream came true, but he lost his future in the process. Now, looking back, he wasn't sure it was worth the cost. The girl he loved, whose once beautiful eyes turned cold and sulky under his gaze.

After returning to Willow Springs, his mother filled him in on all that Anna had lost. Her mother, a stillborn nephew, and now her father at the cost of a shunning.

The Old Order Community he left was nothing like he remembered it. Neighbors against neighbors, families against families, all split down the middle. Some adhered to past traditions, while others embraced a more open relationship with Jesus by following the New Order Fellowship.

Even his own family was feeling the strain. His *datt*, set in his ways, was finding it challenging to leave Bishop Weaver's District. At the same time, he and his younger *bruder*, Benjamin, felt encouraged by the younger group of ministers sharing the Word in Bishop Schrock's District.

Stepping away from his Old Order upbringing for a time opened his eyes to a world of believers he never thought possible. He only recently contemplated joining the new Amish church to give his life to Jesus.

But before he could do that, he had to know Anna could accept his past mistakes. God had forgiven him and led him back to Willow Springs, but could he settle here without Anna?

The seatbelt warning chime brought him out of his head and back to the task. "I'll drop you off and then deliver Anna's groceries to her sisters."

Naomi ran a hand over the polished leather seats. "When is Pete coming to pick up the truck?"

"He's bringing a check out to me later this evening. I need to clear my stuff before I sign the title over to him."

"Don't tell your *datt,* but I've enjoyed our grocery runs. He cringes every time you take me somewhere. If you don't miss it, I sure will."

Simon snickered at his mother's fondness for his shiny black Ford 250. "It served its purpose when I was on the fishing circuit, but now that I'm committing myself back to the Amish church, it does nothing but reminds me of my past mistakes."

"Son, I'm thankful you've found your way home every day. I can see a change in you. The peace that you walk with these days overflows me with joy."

Simon sighed, "I wish *Datt* could see the change."

"Give him time. Everything is so raw right now. He has a lot of pressure being an elder in the church. There is much division in our community. He loves his church, but he also loves his boys. He's torn, and realizes if he sides with Bishop Weaver, he'll lose access to many of his friends, his older children, and their families. It's such a heavy burden to bear."

"That's just it, *Mamm.* There is no other way than to follow Jesus. Why can't *Datt* see that?"

Naomi folded her hands on her lap. "He'll follow, I'm sure of it, but we must let that be his decision."

"How can you be so sure?"

"By the long hours he's been spending in his Bible. His strength has always come from his confidence in the Lord and what the Word teaches him. I have no doubt God will speak to him in His own time." Naomi paused and smiled. "Besides, He answered my prayers. Didn't he bring you back to me?"

"*Jah*, He did. But I came back with more than just me. I returned with a pile of problems I need help sorting out."

Naomi tucked her black purse under her arm. "Like I said, we have enough to worry about today; we aren't going to stress over something that tomorrow might or might not bring. We will trust the Lord, and He will show us the way."

Simon tapped his thumbs on the steering wheel. "But I only have a few months before the hearing. I'll lose everything if I can't convince Anna to help me before then."

"Son, when we give God all the praise and glory He deserves, we often discover we can walk peacefully through circumstances that terrify us. This is no different. Let Him change your overwhelmed heart into one overshadowed by His power to change all things for His good."

Simon let out a long breath. "I wish I had your assurance and faith."

"It will come. You haven't walked through enough of your own hardships to put all your faith in His promises yet."

"Enough of my own trials? What do you call the last few months?"

"A test?"

"A test in what?"

"Replacing your fear with God's sovereignty. There is nothing in your life that God allows to happen that He can't work out if you are only willing to trust in His plan."

***

After dropping his mother off at home and heading to Eli and Rebecca Bricker's, his mother's words weighed heavily on his mind. He had to believe God had a hand in everything he'd been through. Especially by placing him back in Willow Springs, surrounded by the people he needed most.

In the few short weeks he'd been home, he discovered a part of himself he thought he'd lost forever. Now, if he could only convince Anna that God had a purpose for sending him away and bringing him back.

Over breakfast that morning, his father examined one of his favorite questions. *How will you spend this most precious day? The choice is yours. Will you spend it living for the Lord or living for yourself?*

In the past, he would let his father's words roll by him, but today, they dug a hole in his heart as big as the void he had since he left Willow Springs.

For years, Simon had supported a biting spirit due to his disobedience. During those years, he made enough money to buy his heart's desires. But his willfulness poisoned his entire outlook until he found himself in the pits of despair, desperate for a way to claw his way back to the life he once knew.

How could the sins of one man affect so many? His resources should have been used for good; instead, they were devoured by sinful wants and desires. And so, a twinge of remorse crept back into Simon's life as clear as Anna's broken spirit.

A flash of blue and black waved him in as he parked his truck alongside the row of full clotheslines in Eli and Rebecca's side yard. Retrieving the box of groceries from the back seat, Simon carried them up the steps and sat them on the floor near the door.

Eli and Rebecca sat side by side on the swing near the end of the covered porch. Eli set the double chair in motion with his foot and questioned, "What brings you out our way?"

"I told Mr. Shetler I'd deliver Anna's groceries."

Rebecca pressed her hand on the side of her protruding middle. "Without Anna?"

Simon furrowed his eyebrows. "She's not here?"

Eli stopped the swing. "*Nee.* The last we saw her, she was heading to the dry goods store."

Rebecca stood and made her way to the box on the floor. "Why on earth would she need these delivered? It certainly wasn't too much to carry."

Simon lifted his hip and balanced himself on the porch railing. "I suppose I'm to blame. She had a spell at Shetler's, and I tried to help. I planned on bringing her home, but she ran off before I could stop her."

Rebecca pulled her shawl tighter. "Oh, my! Not another one. She's been having more of them lately, and we aren't sure what to do about them." Rebecca exhaled. "This is my fault. I pushed her to step out of the house this morning, hoping a little fresh air and a change of scenery might do her some good."

Eli moved to Rebecca's side and said, "I'm sure she will be home shortly. She probably went for a walk by the creek like she always does."

The mention of their favorite spot along Willow Creek made Simon excuse himself without as much as a goodbye. "I know where she is!"

Gravel flew as Simon backed his truck out of the driveway and headed toward Willow Bridge Road. The only place in Lawrence County where Anna could be is the one place where they confided all their hopes and dreams for the future. He knew it well since he was prone to retreat to the same spot when life became too much to bear, much like every night for the past three weeks.

CHAPTER 2

Anna stayed hidden in the barn's shadow until Simon's truck pulled away. Her heart pounded as she recited Psalm 23. There weren't many things that would calm her racing pulse, but *The Shepherd's Psalm* at least helped put her mind back in line with where she wanted her heart.

As the black truck disappeared over Eli's hill, Anna pondered the weighty question that kept her awake nightly. *Why now?* A heaviness in her chest retold of a bitterness still wedged tight to the point of suffocation. *Oh, Lord, please lay forgiveness in my heart.* Anna turned away with a heavy heart and walked to the yarn shop.

The mailman had left an order on the porch of *Stitch n' Time*, and Anna carried it inside. Her sister Rebecca's husband,

Eli, had finished building their new shop across the yard from the main house last year.

The burden of moving the store away from her father's furniture shop had been a stressful project. If it hadn't been for Eli's persistence, their little yarn shop would cease to exist. Since their church district split, her family endured so much division, but Eli and Rebecca stayed hopeful in God's plan. If only she could have such faith.

No sooner had she unpacked the order of needles and patterns then Rebecca waddled in the door.

"I've been worried sick about you. Simon delivered the groceries I sent you after."

"*Jah*, I saw."

Rebecca pressed her hand on her lower back and settled on the stool at the work table. "*Schwester*, we need to find a solution to your episodes. I will need your help with little Mary Ellen and the new *bobbli*. What are we to do if you can't even handle the shopping? Let alone running the shop by yourself for a few weeks."

Anna lifted her head. "I'll do my best." Bending back over her task, Anna remained silent for a few moments. Then she spoke with some hesitation. "I won't let you down, I promise."

Rebecca tied a price tag onto a set of knitting needles. "Eli and I think you need to get out more. Perhaps face some of your fears of being out in public."

Anna snapped, "I get out plenty."

"I hardly count church every other week as getting out."

"But where else do you expect me to go?"

"To start, you can go back to Shetler's."

Anna's voice was quiet. "Please, not there. I made such a scene this morning."

Rebecca reached out and took her hand. "Anna, you're never going to move past this if you don't push yourself. Remember what Eli said about worry and unrest being rooted in unbelief?"

"But I believe," Anna muttered.

"I'm sure you do, but you've allowed it to become a controlling factor in your life. I think your episodes have become a habit for you."

Anna drew a quivering breath but said nothing. After a moment, Rebecca probed, "Did this morning have anything to do with seeing Simon?"

"*Nee*, I didn't even know he and his mother were in the store until Naomi laid her hand on my shoulder."

"Then what was it? What triggered it this time?"

In a broken voice, Anna replied, "I don't know what's wrong with me. I have no rhyme or reason for what causes them or when I'll have one."

Rebecca walked to Anna's side and wrapped her arm around her shoulder. "I believe that worry, stress, and fear are closely related. If you can figure out what is going on in your head, you might be able to find some peace and confidence in this season of life."

Anna said nothing and left her sister's embrace. "I best put this order away, and I have two buckets of fiber soaking in red cabbage I need to rinse out."

Rebecca headed to the door. "Perhaps a cup of peppermint tea would help, *jah*?"

Anna nodded and smiled at her *schwester's* suggestion. "Might be just what I need to soothe my unsettled nerves."

"If Mary Ellen isn't up from her nap yet, I'll bring you a cup."

After she was sure Rebecca had made it off the porch, Anna fell to a stool and rested her chin in her propped-up palms. She tried to push Simon from her mind by covering her eyes with her fingertips. Strangely enough, she was sure her heightened anxiety attacks had everything to do with Simon's return.

***

Simon pulled his truck alongside the covered bridge in the same spot he and Anna had met every Sunday night for two years straight. A vague resentment began to take root in his heart, taking him back to the night he told Cora he didn't love her. How did he let the *Englisch* girl fall in love with him? He chastised himself for allowing it to happen on more than one occasion. Cora's tear-stained face tugged at his better judgment when he allowed his defenses down and gave in to her desire.

In all the time he'd been toying with the *Englisch* life, there was no doubt he wouldn't return to Anna, the one girl who held his affection, even at the cost of hurting Cora.

The thought of traveling the long road ahead without Anna never crossed his mind until that morning. The look of disappointment etched on her face was a disturbing element.

He wandered to the creek bank and skipped a rock across the rippling water. As the flat stone sank to the bottom, he cried out. God, where are you? I've hurt many people and have not done well with everything you've provided. Please help me make things right. And if it's your will, please soften Anna's heart toward me.

After an hour, he stepped back into his truck and headed home. Catching a glimpse of himself in the rearview mirror, his ball cap and blue t-shirt reminded him it was time to leave the life where money and fame meant more to him than securing his future with Anna.

In a few hours, the last remnant of his old life would pull out of his parent's driveway, leaving him no other option but to embrace his future, with or without the girl he loved. And soon, there would be no hiding his past mistakes. His only prayer was to be able to persuade Anna to help him carry the responsibility together.

Simon drew a long breath as he parked his truck beside his best friend Pete's old pickup truck in front of his mother's kitchen garden.

Both Pete and his younger brother stood next to the dusty Dodge. Pete nodded in his direction as he stepped out of his truck. "You're early. I haven't had a chance to clean my stuff out yet."

"No hurry. My kid brother was headed out this way to pick up a load of grain from the Feed & Seed, so I hitched a ride with him." Pete bounced a closed fist on the bed of his truck. "I convinced Jr. that this old girl had plenty of life left in her, and I'd sell it to him cheap."

Simon threw back his head and laughed. "I sure hope you don't expect me to do the same for you."

"Easy," retorted Pete promptly. "A truck as fine as that one comes at a hefty price; one I'm prepared to pay. You have nothing to worry about there. I'm grateful you gave me first dibs."

Pete's younger brother walked around the glossy fiberglass and ran his hand over the hood. "I'm not sure I'd be able to give something like this up in exchange for a smelly horse and buggy."

Simon took his hat off and ran his hand through his hair. "I've had my fun with it. It's time to let it go. Besides, my brothers have shouldered my share long enough. It's only fair I take back some of the responsibility of running this farm."

Pete rested his foot on the hitch. "What about the boat? Found a buyer yet?"

"Yep, already sold. Along with the house on Lake Erie. The new owner was happy to make it part of the deal."

Pete slapped Simon on the shoulder. "Dang, brother, you must be raking in the dough about now."

Simon was surprised at Pete's outburst. "Means nothing to me now."

"How can you say that? You worked hard for every penny. There are guys on the fishing tour dreaming of earning what you did."

After a second of silence, during which Simon contemplated his response, he justified. "It all came at too high of a cost."

"Come on, buddy, you can't tell me you didn't enjoy everything that came from winning two consecutive Bass Master Classics. You had sponsors eating out of your hand, and every chick this side of the Mississippi pined for your attention."

The muscles in Simon's jaw twitched at the mention of how he basked in the afterglow of stardom. He'd trade every ounce of it if it meant he could regain Anna's trust.

Pete turned toward his younger brother. "You should have seen it. The red carpet was rolled out for bass fishing's wonder boy everywhere we went. The news media ate him up. He was all over the papers and on every fishing channel with...*Amish Boy Wins Professional Bass Tour.*"

Simon opened the tailgate and pulled labeled plastic totes and rods from the bed. "Do either of you have any use for these?"

"You're not going to sell all your fishing gear, are you?" Pete inquired.

Simon handed Pete his favorite drop-shot rod. "I won't have much time to spend on the lake and I'll be lucky to make it to the creek between chores and my job at the lumber mill."

Pete balanced the rod against the truck and picked up a crankbait pole. "You won your last tournament with this rod. Man, are you sure you want to sell these?"

Simon removed the hook from the eye at the tip of a rod and turned away from the truck. After quickly releasing the bail, he sent the spinner bait across the grass. With a quick adjustment to the drag, he reeled it back in, securing the lure back in place. "Like I said, I have no use for them, and I'm done with that part of my life. Besides, most of this tackle was given to me as part of my sponsorship."

Jr. picked up a couple of the rods and carried them to his truck. "If Pete doesn't want them, I'll take 'em."

"Now hold on there; I didn't say I didn't want them; I just said it was a waste that he's giving them away. What if he wants to get back into bass fishing again?"

"That's not going to happen, so take what you want. Perhaps you can donate the stuff you can't use to the kid's fishing program."

Pete pushed the stuff back into the bed of the truck. "I'll do that. I'm sure the kids would love this stuff."

"But what about me? I'm a kid at heart." Jr. grabbed a tackle box full of plastic worms.

"We'll go through everything later. You best get that load of grain before Dad has my tail for keeping you so long. I'll be home as soon as Simon and I take care of some business."

***

Once Pete pulled away from the house, Simon only allowed himself a split second of pain before he pushed the truck from his mind. Heading to the barn, he was genuinely glad to be home. He hadn't realized how badly he had missed his family and the camaraderie he enjoyed with his *bruders*. It was good to expel his energy working the farm.

However, along with the contentment, Simon felt a restlessness about the state of his relationship with Anna. So many things about the farm reminded him of all the plans he and Anna had made. The dream of building a house in the north pasture to opening an herb farm reminded him of all he had lost.

His brother, Ben, handed him a pitchfork the minute he walked through the barn door and went to work cleaning a stall. Simon pondered his father's statement as he piled wet straw in a wheelbarrow...*A man isn't fit to be a husband until he learns to put the Lord first in all he does. You can't raise a family until you foster yourself in God's image.*

"I'm no sooner fit to be a husband than a father," Simon whispered. "What would *Datt* do in my shoes?" There wasn't a doubt he knew precisely what he would do, and that evening, Simon bowed his head over his Bible.

***

The bell above the door jingled, and Anna followed the sound to the front of the shop.

"Naomi, you shouldn't be here. You know we're not allowed to do business together. You'll be under the *bann* yourself if Bishop Weaver gets word."

Mrs. Kauffman walked to the counter. "The way I see it, I have no other place to buy yarn, so I have no other option. And like I said the other day, you let me worry about the bishop. I'm the least of his worries."

Anna lifted her chin and posed a question. "How so?"

Naomi leaned in close. "The Lord is working his way through the community and my husband. Our boys have raised serious questions that have him looking for some biblical answers. You mark my word; this nonsense of separating families will be a thing of the past. I'm praying that your father and the other ministers will see the light soon."

"Okay," replied Anna with a show of assurance she didn't feel. Her father took his position as minister seriously, and she doubted he'd change his stance on their ex-communication. It had been two years since they walked away from their Old Order Community to join the New Order Fellowship. Anna highly doubted her *datt* and the other ministers would ever consider anything else.

Anna hung a new supply of pink wool yarn on a hook and asked, "What can I do for you today?"

Mrs. Kauffman pulled a magazine from her purse. "I found this pattern in my knitting magazine and want to try it. It calls for two skeins of high-quality wool yarn."

"Do you have a color in mind?"

Naomi pulled her glasses from her bag and pushed them up on her nose while examining the rows of muted colors. "Something different, maybe a color no one else has seen."

Waving Mrs. Kauffman to follow her to the back room, she said, "I rinsed out a batch of yarn this morning that I had soaked in salt and red cabbage."

Naomi admired the roving hanging on the rungs of the wooden rack. "How long before the fiber is ready to spin?"

Anna felt the fiber. "It will take twenty-four hours to fully dry and a day to spin. I could have it ready in a couple days. Do you like this color?"

"*Jah*, it reminds me of the lavender I once grew in my garden." The older woman folded her glasses and tucked them back into her bag. "Not sure what happened to it. It won't bloom anymore."

Anna's eyes twinkled while she considered what the problem might be. "Was it English Lavender? That lavender is the only kind that does well here in our hard winters and is hardier than the others."

"*Jah*, I think so."

"Did you trim it back as soon as it stopped flowering?"

"*Nee*, I didn't know it needed that."

"Typically, it blooms in June and July. After that, you need to cut it back, but don't go too far into the wood. Just clip off the dead blooms."

Anna paused. "Where did you have it planted?"

"I planted it under the window in hopes of being able to smell it all summer long."

Anna picked up a pencil and drew the outline of Simon's mother's house on a pad near the register. "Remind me where your gardens are planted."

"I had Ben till up a new garden bed between the barn and the house in the spring."

"If you had it under the living room window where it gets the most sun in the morning, that is northeast. If you moved it to your new area, it would receive more sun in the afternoon since it faces southwest."

Mrs. Kauffman patted Anna's hand. "I'd forgotten how much you loved gardening. Do you think if we move it, it will come back?"

"Have you noticed any green on it? You might be able to save it if you move it right away."

"I haven't looked at it lately. Perhaps you could come to help me?"

She looked out the window, hoping Naomi wouldn't catch the spasm of pain fluttering across her face with the mention of visiting the Kauffman farm. Stuttering, she uttered, "I, I...don...don't think I could get away. Rebecca's baby is due anytime now, and I'm busy here."

Anna resumed her work diligently, trying to ignore the disappointment fixed on Mrs. Kauffman's face. The older woman evidently hoped her answer would have been different, since she had no daughters of her own. No matter, there wasn't an ounce of her that would agree to help. Just the thought of running into Simon made her chest constrict.

Naomi must have sensed her reluctance and said, "On your own, you'll never be able to face your fears. But if He calls you to face what frightens you, He'll give you the strength to live through it."

As the woman headed to the door, another message Minister Yoder mentioned came to mind. *Fear imagined can be put to death by the Spirit and faith.*

Naomi called over her shoulder. "I'll be back for that lavender yarn in a few days."

The woman's sweet voice carried a memory she had long forgotten. Naomi provided wise words to get her through her grief when her mother died, and Anna replayed them in her head. *Anna, our heavenly Father knows exactly what we need when we need it. We can't run ahead of him, hoping to lead the way. Some things are too hard to comprehend, and He knows this. He will only give us what we need for the day. Beyond that, we tell Him we don't have faith if we question our future.*

Anna sunk to the floor, rested her head on her knees, and prayed. *Lord, I want to put all my faith in you. I don't want to be fearful, and I want to face my fears. If only I could figure out what those might be. Please show me how to quit living in the past and fearing the future. Amen.*

Before she lifted her head off her knees, a vision of Shetler's Grocery came to mind. The image played over in her head as she saw herself facing her first fear.

CHAPTER 3

R ebecca sat at the table peeling potatoes when Anna came in to help with dinner. A cup sat at Anna's place with a tea infuser seeping dried peppermint leaves in hot water. She smiled at her sister and added a spoonful of sugar, stirring it slowly while she took in the calming aroma.

"I had Eli stop at Yoder's Bakery this morning to check on the peanut brittle inventory. Emma asked if we would like to join her and Katie for a *schwester's* day tomorrow afternoon. I thought Mary Ellen and Katie's daughter Elizabeth could play while we visit. Would you like to join us?"

Rebecca went on. "Now, before you say a word, I don't think closing the yarn shop early is a problem. Everyone is busy cleaning out their gardens and has little time for yarn shopping."

Anna grabbed her mug with two hands and blew over the hot liquid. "Not sure I'll have much to add to the conversation since you and Katie will be comparing notes on your growing middles."

"Isn't it amazing how we're all with child simultaneously?" Rebecca mused. "Besides, I'm certain it won't be long before you and Emma start your own families."

"Hm, I highly doubt that."

Rebecca snickered. "Those who protest too loudly."

"The only thing to protest is there isn't anyone I'd even consider marrying in this county."

Rebecca carried the pan of potatoes to the sink. "By the way Simon came here looking for you the other day; I'd beg to differ."

For the first time, Anna began questioning her reasoning behind ignoring his persistence in speaking to her. What she needed to do was set him straight. Perhaps facing him would stop some of the anxiety associated with his return and end any hope he might have about their future.

Drawing in a long breath, Anna looked up and met Rebecca's grin. "Whatever you thought you saw in his visit is nothing, I promise you."

"Well, I'd say fate has intervened in your plans."

Anna moved to the stove to check on the roasting chicken. "Fate has nothing to do with it. He practically left me at the altar; I'm not allowing myself to relive that pain ever again."

Rebecca pulled a stack of plates from the cupboard and said, "You need to stop focusing on the past. You've already conjured up the worst-case scenario before giving God a chance to show you what He has in store." Her eyes flashed as she continued, "Remember *Mamm* telling us perfect peace comes to those whose mind is fixed on trusting God?"

Anna plopped down in a chair and sighed. "I trust God; I don't trust Simon."

Rebecca added, "Look, I'm probably not the right person to tell you about trusting the Lord. But I'm not as stressed when I concentrate on just the day in front of me instead of the days before me. Eli told me that trust in God grows as we become more familiar with Him. Maybe He is using your nervousness to draw you closer to Him."

"Maybe. All I know is I've been struggling with controlling my circumstances. With Simon around, I feel vulnerable, which is terrifying."

"I'd say you might need to face that challenge head-on."

"Easier said than done by one who doesn't break out in a cold sweat at the thought of leaving the house," Anna muttered.

"Allowing yourself time away from this farm is exactly what you need. And you can start right after dinner by going back to Shetler's and getting the rest of the groceries I sent you for the other day."

Anna didn't dare argue with her *schwester*. Especially since the store's image weighed heavy on her mind since her earlier cry to God.

***

The forenoon sun beat through the kitchen window as Anna finished the last of the dinner dishes. With their lunchtime meal finished, Mary Ellen tucked in for a nap, and Rebecca resting from the morning chores, Anna was free to go back to the dry goods store. Playing Eli's words in her head, she took a moment to take a cleansing breath before stepping off the porch.

Anna, God doesn't want you to put your trust in your own abilities; he wants you to trust Him. Fear is the devil's playground. Satan wants you to be anxious because you're telling God you don't have confidence in Him when you give in to those emotions.

She respected Eli and was encouraged by his wisdom. He had become her voice of reason as of late, and she used his words to get the courage to return to Shetler's.

She took the shortcut through her father's farm and prayed he was busy in his shop and wouldn't notice. Since leaving her father's church, she was forbidden to see or speak to him or her stepmother, Wilma.

She didn't regret stepping away from her Old Order upbringing. Still, when missing her father became too much to bear, she had to remember what Jesus gave up by saving her. Her daily prayer was that God would touch her father's heart and open his eyes to find salvation in Christ, not a set of rules and traditions.

A shower of yellow and gold leaves fluttered before her as she made her way along the row of maple trees that separated the Yoder and Byler farms. The path weaved its way past her brother Matthew's farm, around the dormant strawberry fields, and landed at the banks of Willow Creek.

The flock of Jenny Wrens perched high in the willow tree released a chatter as she passed. Their bubbly song made her smile as she spotted the feast awaiting them at the creek's edge. Slowing her steps, she rounded the corner and stopped at the covered bridge.

Many memories clouded her vision, forcing her to find comfort on a nearby log. Slipping off her shoes, she dipped her toes in the cool water and reminisced about a day much like today but a few years earlier.

Falling in step with Simon, she walked at his side along the winding path that led to Willow Creek. Simon sat his fishing vest and pole at his feet and pulled her down to join him on a fallen log. Reaching for the small plastic box from the vest pocket, he tied a new hook to the end of the line.

Holding up a jar of chartreuse trout bait, he bid, "So do you think they'll bite on this? Or should I give this yellow and brown rooster tail a try?"

She considered the two, then said, "I like that shiny gold thing on the back, so go with the rooster tail. Maybe the sun will reflect off it, and you'll get a good reaction bite."

He tied on the rooster tail and bumped her shoulder with his. "Listen to you, with all that fishing talk. A girl after my heart, for sure and certain."

"That's a start if you're still calling me your girl."

"Why wouldn't I? You're still my girl, right?"

"I wasn't sure since I said some hateful things a couple of weeks ago. And you haven't written to me to let me know otherwise."

Simon released his hold on the lure. "I had a lot of things to think about, and I wanted to give you some time to cool off."

Simon stood and walked over to the edge of the creek. Clicking the bail open, he flipped his rod back and then forward. They watched his lure sail through the air and to the other side of the creek. Letting the line sink for a few seconds, he slowly reeled the lure back, repeating the process over and over for fifteen minutes. His broad shoulders stood firm as he concentrated on watching the line.

"How does your hand feel?" Anna asked from her spot on the log.

Simon twisted his wrist. "I seem to be able to grip the reel tight, but it will take some time to regain my strength. I'm not sure I'll be up for any fluke fishing soon, but it's a good start."

Leaving the log, she moved to his side. "Fluke fishing, what's that again? You've explained it to me once."

A smile encased his face before he eagerly described the technique. "Remember when we went out on Conneaut Lake last year? I used that soft, white plastic minnow with silver specks on it. I swam the lure with a twitch, twitch...paaaauuuusssseeee...twitch...twitch, twitch motion. It takes a lot of wrist action. I'm not sure my hand is up for that yet."

"Oh, now I remember; that was a fun day. We went out for frozen custard on our way home. That was so nice of Pete to come to Willow Springs to get us so you could take me out on your boat."

Simon rubbed his earlobe. "If I remember right, I still have the scar on my ear to show for that little fishing adventure."

"I'm so sorry; I still can't believe I sliced the end of your earlobe with a hook. I told you I had never fished before, so teaching me to cast came with a price."

"Believe me, it was so worthwhile when you caught that four-pound bass. You showed me up that day, even if I got hooked in the process. Let's say that was the day you caught me."

Reeling in his line, he hooked the lure behind an eye on the rod, grabbed her hand, and led her back to the log.

He took off his straw hat, hooked it on his knee, and ran his fingers through his hair. The way he sucked in a deep breath told her he was about to say something important. Turning to face her, he picked up her hands and looked into her eyes. "You understand how much I love you, right?"

Nodding her head, Anna turned her palms over so he could fully grasp her hands. She waited for him to continue.

"I'm sorry I didn't stop by and see you so we could talk this out. You've been so patient with me, and I promised we would get married this fall. Everything didn't go as planned because of my hand, and I didn't know what to do. I had hoped I would get all this fishing out of my blood and be ready to settle down by now. I'm way past Rumspringa age and should be considering raising a family."

He paused, pulled her hands to his lips, and then kissed the back of her fingers. "You're my everything. But once I become baptized, I won't be able to fish as much, and definitely not in tournaments that will pull me away from home." He hesitated before continuing. "I feel like I'm giving up on my dream before seeing it through."

She felt a heaviness in her chest and watched the color drain from his face. Without a word, she pulled her hands from his, stood, and walked away. Tripping over his pole and vest, she *scrambled to catch herself just as he scooped her up and kept her from falling.*

"Wait, don't go; let's talk," he begged, pulling her close. Allowing her head to relax on his shoulder, he rested his chin on her kapp and whispered, "I can't bear the look of disappointment on your face. I've made you wait long enough. Fishing or not, I must choose us, or I'm afraid I'll lose you."

Pushing herself far enough away to put both hands on his chest, she summoned her courage to ask, "Does that mean you'll talk to the bishop and start your baptism instruction? When do you think we can start planning the wedding? Who should we get to be our side sitters?"

"Whoa there, I can only answer one question at a time. I'll talk to the bishop next week. Let me take care of that, and then we can go from there. Is that okay?"

"I'm more than okay with your plan; it's perfect."

The day would be etched in her memory for as long as she lived. His broken promises and leaving in the middle of the night set a series of events that shaped her future…much to her dismay.

The sun glistened on the water cascading over a small waterfall in the swell of the pebble-lined creek. Sifting through the rocks near her feet, she found a flat rock and skipped it across the water. Everything she did these days reminded her of Simon.

Pulling herself off the bank, she slipped on her shoes and stockings and pushed Simon and his broken promises from her mind. Climbing the bank leading to South Main Street Extension, Anna savored the peaceful stroll by the gentle stream. However, the closer she got to Shetler's Grocery, the journey resembled a wild sled ride down Eli's Hill. Her heart thumped as if her sled ride was on a collision course with a tree with every step.

A lump settled in her throat as she approached the door. An *Englisch* couple with loaded arms pushed their way through the door, forcing her to the corner of the building. The beat in her ears drowned out her shallow breaths as she forced herself to the door again. Overcome with nausea, she retreated to the shadows muttering, "*I will never leave you nor forsake you; I will never leave you nor forsake you; I will never leave you nor forsake you.*"

Her feet moved without any regard for her wish to stay hidden. A row of brightly colored birdhouses and small wooden wheelbarrows used for planters lined the store's porch and helped her make a slow approach. Frozen to the ground at the entrance, a voice uttered, "Don't let your imagination feed your fear."

Wood dust and hard work filled her nose as Simon's hand reached around and opened the waiting door. An irresistible wave of anxiety engulfed her when she stepped through the threshold. His breath tickled the back of her neck as he followed her inside. A stack of wooden baskets prohibited her from making a quick escape when their handles twisted together in the folds of her dress, tipping the pack to the floor.

Simon stepped in front of her, knelt to align the stack, and handed her a single basket. A fine mist of wood shavings covered his arms, which she tried to focus on rather than his face. Their knuckles met, and the lump in the back of Anna's throat dislodged, letting a small sigh escape.

Simon stood, blocking her way. "It's good to see you out and about."

She tried to step around him. "I must go."

"Anna, there'll come a time when you'll have to give me a few minutes."

"*Nee*. We have nothing to talk about." His hand landed on her elbow. "Please, Anna, let me explain."

Her quiet voice broke with a few ending words as if his presence brought a new grasp of all she'd lost. "Time for defending your actions has long passed."

Simon lifted his heart in prayer for direction before he spoke again. "I've been lonely without you in my life."

Anna pulled away. "Whose fault is that but your own?"

Simon was ashamed as she walked away. Turning in the opposite direction, he headed to find the blackstrap molasses his *mamm* needed for shoofly pie, swallowing hard against her statement. While he knew she only spoke the truth, it was still hard to hear.

Anna waited until she turned to the end of the row before putting her hand to her neck and taking a few cleansing breaths. Her palm, moist from their closeness, felt warm to her skin. His mere presence rattled her, and there was no denying their hearts were still intertwined no matter how she wished otherwise.

She peered over a row of cereal boxes, waiting for Simon to leave the store. With all the worry of another anxiety attack behind her, she reached for Rebecca's list in her purse. Peanuts and corn syrup were clearly marked off; she scanned the items while keeping a close eye on the top of Simon's hat...only releasing her breath after he paid Barbara, the cashier, and left.

***

Simon stopped at his horse's head, pulling the brim of his hat down to block the early afternoon sun. Gazing at the storefront, he waited and tightened the bridle before running a hand over the horse's dark mane. One last look before he headed back to work. He hoped to etch her small frame behind his eyes long enough to carry him through another day.

***

Later that afternoon, Simon settled back into his job at Mast Lumber Mill. The hard work did little to clear Anna from his mind as sweat roosted between his shoulder blades. His triceps, still tense from catching slabs of wood at the bottom of the conveyor belt, flexed when he closed his hands around the rough lumber. Even the never-ending pile of boards lurching at him did little to tire his troubled soul. The only thing that kept him going was knowing the extra money he made as a sawyer would come in handy when it came time to prove to Anna that he wasn't leaving again.

When the conveyor belt finally rolled to a stop, he took off his straw hat, brushed aside damp hair from his forehead, and thought, *No matter how long it takes, I'll continue to whittle away at her heart until all my bad choices and shattered dreams break away, making room for a future. No sense in upsetting her further. I'll keep finding ways to see her, even if it means going out of my way to be in her path. One of these days, I'll wear her down enough; she'll have no choice but to listen.*

CHAPTER 4

S imon carried a cup of coffee to the front porch and sat in a willow-bent rocker next to his mother. With the evening meal and evening chores complete, he could rest. Holding the cup in one hand, he laid the other work-worn hand on his knee and sat silently.

With her bare foot, his mother pushed her chair into motion and said, "I've been watching you, and you're troubled. What is it, son?"

"What makes you think so?" Simon took a sip of his sweet cream coffee and lingered at the rim of his cup.

"Mothers are tuned in to the turmoil of their children."

He answered slowly as he set his cup on the stand between them. "I didn't think getting Anna's attention would be so hard."

An evening breeze blew past them, and Naomi pulled her sweater tighter. "You broke her heart. You can't expect her to step back into your life at your beck and call."

"But *Mamm*," he said, "I don't have much time."

Mrs. Kauffman had to smile at his boyish impatience.

"Surrender."

Simon thought it over, then continued, "How much more do I have to surrender? I've sold everything I had, met with Bishop Schrock about starting instruction classes, and asked God to forgive me more times than I thought possible."

His mother stood and rested her hand on his shoulder. "Could be you're putting something before Him." Raising an eyebrow, she continued, "Or perhaps you're trying to pry a door open He's not ready for you to walk through yet."

She walked to the door and stopped. "Have you been seeking guidance from above? Or have you been relying on your own understanding of what troubles you?"

Simon gripped the chair arms and stared out at his father's dairy farm. Finally, he reacted, unsure if he could express what troubled him most.

"As Christians, we are to forgive, correct?"

"*Jah*. Why?" His mother requested.

"I don't think Anna can get over my betrayal." Simon stayed quiet until his mother spoke. "You are underestimating the power of prayer."

His voice broke as he answered, *"Jah."*

Simon walked to the barn, hoping to find a spot he could have a quiet word with the Lord. Above, the September sky came to life with tiny lights, and as he looked at them, they seemed closer than Anna was. Folding his arms across the top rail of the corral, he closed his eyes and buried his head in his joined arms.

Later in his room he rose from his knees, the Bible still open on the bed. His eyes stung as thoughts of Anna still swirled around. But now, a new warmth of peace surrounded him as He felt God's hand in his life. His mother was right; he had put God's plan above his desires, and just admitting it and asking for forgiveness helped calm his restless mind.

Shutting his Bible, Simon crawled into bed and prayed one last prayer. *"Lord, whatever the cost, I lay this at your feet. Bless Anna and bring us closer if that is your will. Amen."*

***

The following day was full and busy for Anna. She worked from early morning until it was time to help Rebecca with dinner. She hoped all thoughts of Simon would be lost to occupied hands.

After taking a yarn inventory, she set a pot on the propane heater to boil a batch of avocado pits. The all-natural vegetable colorant would turn the white alpaca hair a lovely shade of peach. While the dye simmered, Anna soaked the fiber in a vinegar and water solution that would help set the color of the fiber.

With Naomi's lavender yarn complete, she placed it on the worktable and wrote up a receipt before moving to the spinning wheel on the front porch. While the weather was pleasant, she loved to spin yarn outside, allowing remnants of the fine fiber to float away with the wind.

The clean fiber was silky as she twisted it while pumping the pedal with her foot. After adjusting the tension, she set her foot back steadily as she drew the rope roving back and forth, feeding it on the bobbin. She enjoyed working with alpaca fiber the most, unlike the prickly sheep's wool.

Her back to the driveway she continued to work to fill the bobbin. Typically, it would take her five hours to work through a basket of roving, but today, she only had a short time.

An orange-top buggy pulled up to the hitching post, but she didn't take her eyes off the twisted fiber flowing from her fingers. When she finally slowed the wheel with her hand, Anna looked up, a little frown puckering her brow.

Simon tipped his hat. "Anna."

Her gut twisted, and she snapped, "What do you want now?"

With a grin of determination, he declared, "We live in the same community, so you best get used to me being around."

Anna set the wheel in motion and continued to wind the thin fibers through her fingers. "Why are you here?"

"*Mamm* asked me to stop and check on her yarn order."

The wheel slowed, and she folded the loose roving in her lap apron and set it aside. "I'll get it for you."

She longed for him over the years, which sometimes seemed unbearable. Now he was so close, and all she wanted was for him to disappear. But at every turn, he kept showing up. She would need to stop it, and quickly if she was going to get any peace.

Anna stepped behind the work table, trying to formulate a plan. "Next time, tell your mother she can call the phone shanty and leave a message. I can easily drop an order in the mail."

Anna held her breath as Simon sighed. "The mail? I'd say that's a tad ridiculous. Why would you waste good money on postage when we live so close?"

"It would save you a trip."

"Did you happen to think I might enjoy seeing you?"

Her lips set in tight. "Did you think I'd much rather not see...*you*?" With shaky hands, Anna tore the receipt from the pad and stuffed it with Naomi's order in the bag. The words stung as soon as they left her lips. When she handed him the brown sack, he took her hand and said, "You can continue to push me away, but you won't be able to stop my prayers."

He dropped her hand before she had a chance to pull away. Leaving her to study his troubled face, she couldn't help but wonder what exactly he was praying for. His eyes didn't hold anger at her harsh treatment, but the softness in his voice spoke of hope.

After he left, she glanced at the time, gathered her supplies from the porch, and locked the shop. Emma and Katie were expecting them for their *schwester* day.

***

Rebecca handed Mary Ellen to Anna before stepping out of the buggy carrying a covered casserole dish. As soon as Anna followed Rebecca, the toddler squirmed out of Anna's arms and ran toward Elizabeth playing in the sandbox in the sideyard. Emma and Katie waved them to the picnic table under the autumn-filled maple tree.

Emma rushed to her waddling *schwester's* side and emptied her arms. "By the way it looks, Mary Ellen will have a new playmate any day now."

Rebecca pushed a kick from her ribcage and lowered herself to the bench. "I'm much bigger than I was with Mary Ellen; I'm sure Eli is getting a new little farm hand with this one."

Anna stood next to Katie and asked, "Who is minding the bakery?"

"My *mamm* and Barbara Wagler."

"How is Barbara doing?" Anna asked. "It was such a shame her John was taken at such a young age. It breaks my heart that she has to raise those boys without their *datt*."

Emma opened her picnic basket and snapped open a red-checkered tablecloth. "I hear John's older *bruder*, Joseph, found his way back to the fold and is helping her with the farm."

Walking around the table, Emma laid out plates and silverware. She continued, "God has a way of stepping in and laying out a plan in the most mysterious ways. We haven't seen the hide or hair of Joseph Wagler in five years, and out of the blue, he comes back ready to join the church."

Katie took the cover off a bowl of seven-layer salad, laid a spoon across the top, and turned toward Anna. "Much like Simon, *jah*?" Katie gave her arm a squeeze.

Anna stuttered, "I wouldn't know his plans, and I...I don't care."

All three women giggled simultaneously, but it was Rebecca who spoke up. "You can deny you don't care with your lips, but your eyes paint a different picture."

Anna busied herself with folding napkins and securing them under each plate as she drew a deep breath. "I'd prefer not to be the topic of conversation this afternoon if you all don't mind."

Katie sat and rested her arm across her widened middle. "But you're the only one with something exciting to talk about besides dirty diapers and sticky fingers."

"What about Emma? Her life has to be more exciting than mine even if she's not with child."

Emma's face illuminated. "Well, there is something I've been intending to tell you all." She didn't need to say another word as her two *schwesters* and her best friend Katie engulfed her in a hug.

Katie was the first to push back. "I thought you had filled out some, but I figured you'd been tasting too many sweets at the bakery."

Emma slapped her arm and laughed. "Are you trying to tell me I'm getting fat?"

Katie blushed. "You have to admit we do a lot of sampling."

Rebecca asked without thinking, "Have you told *Datt* and Wilma?"

Emma's face dropped. "I thought of sending a note off to him, but I'm sure he'll throw it away without opening it."

"But what if…" Anna's voice trailed off doubtfully.

Emma sighed. "There's no use; Samuel and I have gone round and round trying to figure out a way to tell him he'll have another grandchild." Emma turned toward Rebecca. "I suppose if Mary Ellen or Matthew's girls didn't force him to reconsider his stand on our excommunication, I can't think our child will have much pull either."

Rebecca struggled to swing her leg under the table. "I have to believe if *Mamm* were still alive, she would do everything to be a part of her grandchildren's lives. It sickens me that *Datt* is so fixed on the past he won't even consider doing away with this split."

Anna folded her knee under her hip, rested her chin on her propped-up palm, and asked, "Do you think he misses us?"

Emma took a seat beside her. "I think now that his new minister position has worn off some, he may be second-guessing siding with Bishop Weaver and the old ways.

Samuel has talked to many of our neighbors, and most agree the old ways no longer serve our community. Many believe if the ministers and bishop taught more about Jesus, the way the Bible says, we wouldn't lose so many to the *Englisch*."

Katie reached for a ginger snap. "Daniel mentioned both Joseph and Simon have met with Bishop Schrock about instructional classes."

Emma faced Anna. "That's good news, *jah*?"

"I might as well save you all the trouble of jumping to conclusions," Anna said wearily. "That ship has long sailed."

"Why else would he have come back?" Rebecca's lips turned up.

"Quit! I don't care why he returned, and I'm tired of everyone asking me about him. If you want to know, ask him."

Anna twisted her hands in her lap. "I'm sorry, I didn't mean to sound so sharp. I've had a hard time seeing him. I admit running into him so much has gotten me quite worked up."

Emma wrapped her arm around her shoulder. "Could it be you still have feelings for him?"

"I didn't think I did, but my heart races every time I see him. I can't tell if it's anger or anxiety. I thought I'd forgiven him for leaving two days before our wedding, but the way my stomach lurches every time I see him, I don't think I have."

Rebecca added a scoop of salad to her plate. She waited until they all bowed their heads and looked back up before adding, "He was pretty concerned with your whereabouts last week. The look on his face told me more than anything."

Anna stayed silent as the three girls talked about their upcoming births. While she was happy for Emma and Samuel, especially since they had to wait so long before trying again, a deep sorrow was mulling around her heart. If she looked back on how she thought her life would be by now, children were definitely in the picture.

From across the yard, Katie's mother, Ruth, walked their way carrying Anna's peanut brittle basket. "Anna, I hoped I'd see you today. We can't keep your candy in stock. As soon as we fill your basket, we've sold it all before we notice."

Anna took the straw basket from her hands. "What on earth? I made three batches last week. Who's buying it all?"

"We did have a couple of bus tours stop by this week, but the Kauffman boys are gobbling up most of it. Mainly Simon. When I asked him about it, he said it was one of the things he missed most about Willow Springs."

Anna took a drink of meadow tea and coughed out a mouthful at Ruth's statement. After wiping her chin, she fought back the mental and spiritual battle forging inside.

Ruth bent down and muttered close to Anna's ear. "Before you go home today, come over to the house. I have something I've been meaning to give you."

With a quizzical tilt, she answered, "Sure."

Rebecca and Emma exchanged a glance, and Ruth winked at them most peculiarly.

As Ruth returned to the bakery, Anna asked, "What's that all about?"

Rebecca put a forkful of food in her mouth and talked through the bite. "We can't be sure, but I think we both know what Ruth is up to. Trust me, you'll benefit from doing as she asks."

The girls enjoyed catching up and watching Mary Ellen and Elizabeth play in the yard for the next couple of hours. Emma raked a pile of leaves and taught the girls how to jump and hide in fall glory. While Katie and Rebecca were past frolicking in the grass, Anna and Emma chased the toddlers so much that a nap would come easy for them.

Mary Ellen climbed into Rebecca's lap. "Anna, I'm about ready to head home soon. Do you want to go to Ruth's before we leave?"

"Today is a beautiful day. How about you and Mary Ellen head home? I'll see what Ruth needs, and then I'll just walk."

Anna helped Emma clean the picnic table before heading to Ruth's house. She stopped when she noticed Barbara locking the bakery door and waited for her to walk her way.

Anna looked at her friend's face as she walked to the side of the road. Barbara looked weary. "How are you?"

"*Gut,* I suppose. I'm struggling with working both at Shetler's and the bakery. The bishop does not like it one bit. He keeps saying my place is with the boys, but without John farming, we need to eat and pay the taxes. I don't have much choice."

Anna trod lightly. "I hear Joseph is back and is helping you with the farm."

Barbara dropped her eyes. "I have mixed feelings about his return. I'm trying not to overthink it, but I admit his presence rattles me. He wants to help with the farm, but I haven't given in to his pleas yet."

Anna gasped. "I sympathize with you."

Barbara reached out and rested her hand on her arm. "I heard Simon was back."

The lump in Anna's throat began to break up, and for a moment, she could be honest with someone who understood. "I was just getting used to the fact I needed to move on, and lo and behold, he's back. My anxiety level skyrocketed, and all those old feelings came rushing to the surface. To be quite honest, I wish he'd never come back."

Barbara moved in closer and said, "I feel the same way," with a sob in her voice. "Joseph and I had our future planned, and when he jumped the fence to the *Englisch,* I didn't think I'd ever love again. But then John took his place, and now I must deal with all those old feelings again with John gone and Joseph back."

Anna drew in a long shuddering breath. "Oh, Barbara, what are we to do?"

Her friend seemed to struggle for the right words. "John's *mamm* told me I need to trust in the Lord. She also said the trials we face are not the result of God's inability to see what we need, but a sign of his loving care."

Anna snarled, "But look what they did to us, and we're supposed to be happy with their return?"

"Believe me, I'm trying to work through it as much as you. But relying on God and not my feelings is proving to be a challenge. John's parents have been wonderful and gave me some good advice."

Anna wanted to hear more. "May I ask what advice they gave you?"

Barbara smiled and nodded her head. "Andy is wise, and his words often comfort me. Last night, he reminded me that God is always in control. We play God instead of being godlike whenever we try to sway our circumstances."

Anna swallowed hard. "I keep hearing stuff like that. But boy, is it hard to give up all that control."

"I agree! Well, I best be getting home to the boys. I'm sure my mother-in-law has had enough of those rambunctious grandsons."

Left alone on the side of the road, Anna fought back another wave of anxiousness and struggled to gain a sense of peace in her mind before visiting with Ruth.

CHAPTER 5

Ruth peered out the kitchen window, and her heart pained as she watched the two young women at the end of her driveway. Both girls shared similar struggles, but it was her best friend, Stella's daughter, Anna, who consumed her thoughts. She and Stella made many precious memories during their thirty-year friendship, but the one they shared on her death bed tugged at her the most.

The promise to deliver a special gift to each of Stella's daughters was the one thing that kept her dearest friend's memory alive. Ruth poured two tea glasses and sat at the table, a hand resting on the white dress box she'd carried to the kitchen.

***

Anna continued to steady herself before knocking on Ruth's door. With only the screen between them, Ruth called her in, pulled out a chair, and patted the polished oak seat as she entered the kitchen.

"Sit, child. I have a little something I've wanted to share with you." Ruth pulled the box closer and slid it in front of Anna.

"Your mother asked me to share this with you when I felt you needed her the most. I've been watching you the last few weeks and thought this might help bring her closer."

The corner of Anna's lip quivered with the mention of her mother. She lifted the cover off the box and pushed aside pink tissue paper. A light gray crocheted shawl lined the box. Pulling the soft yarn to her cheek, she closed her eyes, hoping a vision of her mother would appear.

Ruth stood and laid a hand on her shoulder. "Take as much time as you need. I'll be out in the garden if you want to talk."

Anna placed the garment across her lap and ran her fingertip over her mother's perfect penmanship on the envelope left for her. A ripple of emotion landed on her nose as she opened her mother's letter.

My Dearest Anna,

From the time you came into this world, on Rebecca's heels, your quiet spirit brought a sense of peace to our family. To that, I will always be grateful for your gentle ways.

If you're reading this letter, Ruth has followed my wishes and presented you with this small gift. She will have only shared this with you when you needed some of my guidance. Please take my words to heart and apply them to the challenges you face today.

Accept this present and wrap it tightly around your shoulders whenever you need to feel me close. With every stitch, I prayed for you and your future. And even though I cannot walk through life with you, I've poured my heart out to the one who can.

Rest assured, God holds today and all of your tomorrows in the palm of His hand. The peace He offers you is beyond your understanding and is better than ever imagined. I promise that if you turn to Him, He will guard you against falling into the depths of despair.

Having to face the end of my life, I've learned much about trusting God. Not only did I have to surrender the care of my children, but I had to admit I couldn't control the outcome of my tomorrow.

Anna, you tend to worry first and trust second. I know these things because I've struggled with the same. It wasn't until I started to go to God in prayer that I truly understood how important it was to pray with gratitude.

When God instructed us not to worry, He didn't say we wouldn't face challenges. Instead, He wants us to focus all our energy on being thankful. When those troubling thoughts make their way into our minds, we can say: "I'm not going to think about that because I've already prayed about it."

Are you going to God in prayer, Anna? Are your thoughts causing you to be fearful? Go to Him in prayer and ask for all things. Then walk away and let Him do what He does best...filling your heart with courage and a solid commitment to follow Jesus. Find your happiness in Him; He will guide your path if you let Him.

One last thing.

Your datt will need you all when I'm gone, for one, you'll need to do everything in your power to keep the family close. Give him lots of grandbabies and keep him involved in your life.

I pray he will be surrounded with love and family until he comes to meet me at heaven's pearly gate.

Until we meet again,

Mamm

Anna cried for a few moments before she folded the letter and tucked it beneath the layers of tissue paper. It was like a knife thrust through her heart at her mother's request about her father.

The life her mother wished for would never be with their lovely community split between old and new. Her father on one side, and she and her siblings on the other. As it stood, he had never held Rebecca and Eli's daughter Mary Ellen. He had only seen her brother Matthew's two girls as infants.

She cried, "My Lord, what am I to do?"

Tucking the dress box under her arm, she headed to the garden where Ruth filled a wheelbarrow with the last of the ripe tomatoes. Anna sat at the garden's edge and balanced her gift on folded knees.

Anna looked over the garden long before saying, "I've failed *Mamm,* and I'm sure I've disappointed God."

Ruth emptied her hands and moved to Anna's side, kneeling beside her as she put an arm around her trembling shoulders. Anna drew in a long breath at the loving tenderness of her mother's best friend and let herself relax momentarily. Then, remembering her mother's final request, she stiffened again. Ruth let go and picked up Anna's chin with a single finger.

"Whatever it is, it can't be that bad. And besides, God would never be disappointed in you."

"Oh, Ruth, I'm not sure what I should do. *Mamm* asked me to keep the family together and look at us. *Datt's* never held his granddaughter. It's been almost two years since he has seen any of his children. It would break her heart if she knew the state of her family." With difficulty, Anna suppressed the tightness in her throat.

"Anna, I'm sure your mother would be upset, but you must remember we split from a church that didn't allow us to follow Jesus openly. Without a doubt, she would want her children to know Jesus above everything else."

A look of pain settled on Anna's pale face, and she asked, "Did she know Jesus?"

Ruth's eyes smiled, and she patted Anna's folded hands. "Oh, child. It was your mother who showed me the truth. She not only knew, but she shared her new-found love of Jesus with whoever came to visit her in those last few weeks."

"But why didn't she share it with *Datt*? Maybe if she had, he would have walked away from the Old Order with his children."

"She did. But your father wasn't so quick to accept the truth. He begged her not to sway her children. But she's sent all of you a message of her belief in salvation."

"Matthew, Emma, and Rebecca have all received a letter too?"

"Jah."

Anna admired Ruth and loved her dearly when she saw the compassion in her eyes. "You helped her reach us, didn't you?"

Ruth smoothed out her apron. "She would have done the same for me, for sure and certain."

Anna paused, before asking. "How did you get Levi to leave the church so easily?"

"I had nothing to do with it."

"But how so? You're his wife."

"I prayed. God did the rest."

Ruth walked back to the row of tomatoes, but not before adding, "Anna, you need to get out of your head. Once you realize you have no control other than the prayers you petition God for, you'll be happier. Quit trying to line your life up on a tidy little path, and let God lead your way. Even if it means you must step in a mud puddle a time or two along the way."

Anna stood, brushed dried leaves from her apron, and picked up the dress box. "It's been hard to see past what keeps showing up in front of my face."

Ruth peered over the filled wheelbarrow. "Would that happen to be Simon Kauffman?"

After a few seconds of silence, Ruth spoke again. "What are you afraid of?"

Anna's eyes misted over. "I'm trying to trust when it comes to Simon, but the thought of opening my heart again terrifies me."

Ruth stood and balanced her hands on her hips. "So, you'll give up on love in fear of what might happen?"

"The thought of allowing him to become part of my life again is a hard cross to bear."

"Anna, I can't imagine how hurt you were when he left you a few days before your wedding, but you must forgive and move on. If you harbor this pain, you'll never find the peace God offers you. What would have happened if Jesus had walked away from us because it was too hard to do what God asked him to do?"

A peaceful expression flooded Ruth's concerned face when Anna answered. "I think God sent you to remind me of such things."

Anna and her *schwester's* treasured Ruth's motherly influence and love. And they found consolation in her wise words, which always came when needed.

***

As Anna lay in her room listening to an array of nighttime chatter through the open window, she longed to find a way to reach out to her father. Mixed in the pain of her family's separation, she struggled to push Simon's face from her mind. A late-season warmth blew past the curtain and settled on her face as she drifted off to sleep.

***

Simon sat on the edge of his bed, holding a small photo up to the light. The dark-haired baby tugged at his heart as he ran his thumb over the tattered picture and whispered, "I'm working hard to get back to you; please don't grow too fast, my son."

He slipped the photo into his Bible and stretched his feet out on the bed. Clasping his hands under his head, he watched shadows from the oil lamp dance on the ceiling and thought of Anna. Remembering the letter from Cora's parents' lawyer, he swung his feet over the bed and re-read its contents.

The letter contained several things he needed to take care of. A letter of character recommendation from the bishop, a financial statement, proof of employment, and the one thing he prayed for daily, evidence of a stable home life. His son's maternal grandparents required all those things before releasing custody of their only grandchild.

After Cora was killed in a car accident, her parents hesitated to hand over the baby to a man whose reputation followed him through the tabloids.

Six months was such a short time to turn his life around and prove to Cora's parents he could be trusted with the only thing they had left of their daughter…*Marcus*. Anna was the key to showing them the child would be well cared for. Somehow, he had to prove to Anna he was on his way back to her long before Cora stepped into the picture.

On those days when he struggled to forgive himself, Bishop Schrock's words reminded him he was present for every wrong decision. Still, those bad choices didn't define his future if he used them to draw closer to God.

Setting the letter aside, he laid back down and talked to the only one who would listen, His Heavenly Father, who saw all, knew all, and forgave him for his free will.

He prayed and longed to raise Marcus in a home that put God first in all they did. And it never crossed his mind Anna wouldn't love his son. However, the barrier would be, could she love him as she once did?

***

A ray of sunshine warmed Anna's face as she greeted the morning. A small child's face invaded her dreams, and she kept her eyes closed, hoping to focus on the fading memory. Suddenly, she sat up and pushed the image away, chalking it up to spending the day with her *schwesters*.

Mary Ellen's cries called to her through the adjoining wall. She met Rebecca in the hallway, shuffling toward her niece's room.

"Oh, thank goodness you're up." Rebecca had become pale as she steadied herself on the wall.

Calmly, Anna took her by the elbow and led her back to her room. "Go back to bed; I'll take care of Mary Ellen."

Rebecca's voice rose. "I'm nauseous this morning and all crampy."

"You're only at eight months. I think it's too early to be in labor, *jah*?"

Rebecca doubled over and moaned. "I'd say this little one has other plans."

Anna helped Rebecca sit on the edge of the bed. "I'll send Eli to fetch Dr. Smithson. Will you be all right for a few minutes?"

"*Jah*."

Anna scooped Mary Ellen up from her crib and headed to the barn. She found Eli huddled over the workbench. "Eli, I think your little one wants to come a few weeks early."

Eli wiped his hand on a red shop rag. "So soon?"

"*Jah*, I'd say so."

Anna followed Eli to the house, put Mary Ellen in her highchair, and placed a handful of cereal on her tray before checking on Rebecca.

Another long sigh met Anna as Eli helped Rebecca move to the chair under the window. Eli pointed to the wet spot in the center of the mattress. Anna pulled the linens from the bed and said, "I don't think we have time to wait for the doctor; go fetch Ruth."

Eli became white and disappeared without another word. Rebecca snickered between contractions. "He can deliver lambs all day long, but this is too much for him."

"Me too; I'd much prefer the doctor to be here," Anna said slowly as the magnitude of the situation dawned on her.

As another wave moved across Rebecca's middle, she groaned, "Not...you too!"

Anna added a layer of towels over the mattress cover before snapping clean sheets over the bed and heading to her *schwester's* side. "Let's get you back to bed before the next round starts."

Rebecca squeezed Anna's hand. "Oh my, this one's going to be quick."

After Anna got Rebecca settled, she checked on Mary Ellen, filled a sippy cup with milk, and added another handful of round oats to her tray. "You be a good girl. I'll be right back, *jah*?"

Mary Ellen held up a single oat to Anna; she took it and kissed her on the top of her head before returning to Rebecca.

Rebecca cried, "The *bobbli* is coming. Eli needs to hurry with Ruth."

The screen door barely stopped bouncing off its frame before Eli and Ruth arrived in the bedroom. Ruth looked in Anna's direction. "How far apart?"

"One right on top of another."

Ruth shooed Eli out of the room. "Go tend to Mary Ellen; we'll holler if we need you."

Eli bent forward and laid his hand on Rebecca's cheek. "Do you want me to stay?"

Rebecca faltered, then glanced at Ruth, her eyes finally resting on her husband. "No, go. I'm in excellent hands."

After Ruth gave Anna a list of instructions, Anna and Eli moved to the kitchen, leaving Ruth to care for Rebecca.

Eli had taken Mary Ellen from her highchair and had set her on the counter washing her hands.

Anna spoke quietly, taking the warm cloth from his hands. "Ruth thinks it best you go for Dr. Smithson. The *bobbli* might need more than she can handle."

Pausing to steady himself before leaving, Eli took a long look toward the bedroom. "I'll hurry. Pray Anna...pray."

The sounds coming from her *schwester's* bedroom caused her to take Mary Ellen outside as soon as they both dressed. The child threw her arms around Anna's neck with the promise of a piggyback ride.

Setting Mary Ellen in the sandbox, Anna dug her bare feet into the cool sand. She couldn't help but marvel at the look of love she witnessed on her brother-in-law's face. Eli loved Rebecca; there was no doubt about it.

Her mother's letter came to mind about how she had prayed over every stitch, and she assumed she did the same for Rebecca and Emma. The reminder about praying to God and then stepping aside and letting him do what he did best floated through the air. All worry left Anna's mind after she stopped to pray, remembering her mother's words...

He wants us to focus all our energy on being thankful. When those troubling thoughts make their way into our minds, we can say: "I'm not going to think about that because I've already prayed about it."

Ruth's voice rang out from the porch. "Anna, come!"

Anna moved to the house, brushing sand off Mary Ellen's dress, and balanced her on her hip.

Mary Ellen ran toward Rebecca's room when Anna set her down. Running after her, she stopped in the doorway at the sight of the newborn snuggled to Rebecca's chest.

Ruth rolled a stack of towels and picked up a basin. "That little guy must weigh eight pounds and is as healthy as a full-term *bobbli*."

Anna sat on the edge of the bed and pulled Mary Ellen up onto her lap. "A new *bobbli bruder* for you."

Mary Ellen reached for his tiny head, and Anna pulled back her small fingers. "Careful now."

Eli stepped into the room and knelt beside his family. "You just couldn't wait, could you, little guy?"

Anna handed Mary Ellen to her father and stepped out of the room with Ruth and Dr. Smithson. As Ruth and the doctor spoke in the hallway, Anna walked outside.

CHAPTER 6

H ours turned into days as Anna spent every minute caring for her *schwester's* family. Little John Paul found his place in the Bricker family. Even Mary Ellen fell in love with her new *bruder* and woke each morning asking for him.

While Anna enjoyed being an active member of the Bricker household, a void had worked its way into her life. She yearned for a family of her own. In those moments when John Paul slept in Rebecca's arms, the realization she may never have a child of her own left her thinking of Simon and what could have been.

Rebecca stopped her as Anna carried a laundry basket through the living room. "I think I can handle the *kinner* for the afternoon. Why don't you go open the shop for a few hours?"

She saw signs of Rebecca and Eli's happy family in every direction. There was an open Bible, Mary Ellen's toys, John

Paul's baby quilt, and Rebecca's growing happiness. Oh, how she wished she was content.

"Perhaps I shall if you're sure you'll be okay without me."

"Women have been having babies for years, and most don't have their *schwester* living with them. I'm sure I'll be capable."

Anna was lost, not knowing for sure what was bothering her. When she unlocked the door to the yarn shop, she left the screen door open to let the crisp September air fill the room. After opening a window, she sunk down on the stool near the worktable and laid her head on her folded arms.

As soon as she closed her eyes, the small boy from her dream came to mind. Trying to remember the vision that woke her that morning, she brought the child's dark hair and eyes to life. A warmth filled her, and she squeezed her eyes tighter, hoping to keep the scene alive. Behind her eyes, she knelt, welcoming the boy into her embrace as they tumbled back in a field of lavender. His child-like giggles stopped when the door slammed against its hinges. Lifting her head and rubbing the spots from her eyes, she said, "I'll be with you in a minute."

When her eyes cleared, Simon stood twirling his hat in his fingers looking concerned, then he asked, "Did I interrupt a nap?"

"Hardly; I was just thinking, that's all."

"May I inquire as to what has you so perplexed?"

When she lifted her head to meet his eyes, his matted hair left a curled-up ring around his head, and she couldn't help but laugh.

"What's so funny?"

She straightened a stack of patterns. "You look like you have a tire swing around your head."

He ran his hand through his hair. "If that's all it takes to get you to smile, I'll sport an old tire on my head daily."

The light in her eyes faded. "What do you need, Simon?"

He took a note from his pants pocket. "*Mamm* asked me to deliver this to you. I'm to wait for an answer."

After reading its contents, Anna unfolded the flower-lined paper and dropped it in the trash.

Anna,

Help! My lavender plants are dying.

Naomi

"Tell her I'll stop by tomorrow morning."

He didn't say a word, and as if time stood still, they both stared at one another, waiting for the other to break the spell. It was Simon who spoke first. "Can we sit for a minute?"

She pointed to the stool, feeling relatively small next to his towering frame. Her pulse quickened when he laid his hat on the table and pulled the chair closer to her. The emotional struggle her heart and head were having forced beads of sweat to form on the back of her neck.

She pushed her stool away and tucked her hands under her thighs. When he took longer than she felt necessary, she hurried him along. "I have work to do. What is it you want to say?"

He waved her quiet. "Please give me a minute. I want to make sure what I say comes out perfect."

Her knee bounced, and he stopped it with his large hand. She pulled away, allowing his hand to fall. "There was a time when I didn't revolt you."

Her mouth dropped open. "And whose fault is that?"

"Anna, please, you must forgive me. I've made many mistakes and want to make things right."

"I'm not sure that's possible."

He looked up and smiled wearily, making her chest tighten, with his reply, "All things are possible with God."

The once confident young man she fell in love with was looking at her with eyes begging her to hear him out. The edginess she felt when he first sat down melted away with his hopeful tone. She countered, "I'm not sure I have anything else to give. I gave you my heart, and you trampled on it until it barely beat."

He reached for her hands, but she clasped them on her lap, ignoring his desire. "I've forgiven you. That's not the problem."

"Then why won't you let me make it up to you?"

For a second, there was silence, and she was taken back to the letter she had received from his wife over a year ago. The day all hope of his return washed away with her tears. Disappointment lodged in her throat, and she gurgled, "I don't trust you."

Simon's distress hardened his glare, and he dropped his head.

With a gulp of deep emotion, she added, "I'm not sure why you've come back, Simon. Go home to your family. You've made your choice; now live up to your responsibilities."

She left him sitting in the shop and walked back to the house. He made his choice long ago, and no amount of begging or pleading eyes changed that fact. He had broken her heart and walked out on his wife and child. He had no right even talking to Bishop Schrock. With a long sigh, she pushed open the kitchen door, blocking his *Englisch* family from her thoughts.

Anna never shared Cora's letter with anyone and buried the hurt under layers of lost hopes and dreams.

***

Simon waited until he heard the house door close before moving to the porch. He thought he could handle anything she confronted him with, but losing her trust was worse than losing her love. What did she mean by demanding he go home to his family? That is what he had done. He came back to Willow Springs to live up to his obligations.

After a thoughtful pause, Simon stepped up in the buggy and clicked his tongue to direct his horse to the road. A new sense of determination entered the canvas-covered carriage. He vowed to depend entirely on the Lord's lead.

***

Simon found his mother in the basement when he returned home. "Anna said she'd be over in the morning."

"Oh, perfect. If anyone can figure out what is wrong with those plants, she can."

Simon moved a stack of canning jars as his mother swept. The two stayed in thoughtful silence as they cleaned around the jar-lined shelves, which took up one whole side of the basement. Naomi emptied a full dustpan into the trash and spoke slowly. "Give her time. She'll come around, I'm sure of it."

Simon sat on the step and rested his elbows on his knees. "I'm not so sure. She doesn't trust me."

Naomi turned over an old milk crate and took a seat. "I'm sure the Lord is using this healing time to help the both of you shape your future."

"I'm not sure we have much of one, but I am leaving it up to Him to figure it out."

"You wouldn't have found your way back to us unless there was a reason you were meant to be here. Have patience in God's timing."

"But Cora's parents won't give me Marcus unless I can prove he'll be raised properly. In my books that means both a *mamm* and *datt*."

"Simon, you must remember his grandparents are in their sixties and in no position to raise a child. I am confident he'll be reunited with you when God sees fit and not one moment before."

He reached for his mother's aging hand and helped her up. "Thank you," he said warmly.

***

A mix of clouds and sun met Anna as she walked through the covered bridge and onto Willow Creek Road. The three-mile walk to the Kauffman farm gave her ample time to contemplate her life, or the lack thereof, as her mood indicated.

Pushing through an overwhelming heaviness, the closer she got to Naomi's house, the more she begged God to help her trust Him instead of her own feelings. *Lord, I want to obey you and follow your path for me, whatever it might be. Please help me see you in every part of my life and help me understand why you've placed Simon back in my path. No matter how fearful I feel, I want to be strong in you. I'm nothing without you. I want to grow in my faith and not be foolish in understanding your plan. Help me rise above my past and live solely in your present. Amen.*

A light rain speckled the road as Simon pulled up beside her.

"That dark cloud is about to let loose. Best let me take you to the house."

Anna looked to the sky and back to Simon. "I'm fine."

"Dag gone-it, Anna. Quit being so stubborn and get in."

The rise of Simon's chest forced her to walk in front of the buggy and climb inside. He had both sides of the canvas rolled up, allowing the rain to find its way to her face. Pulling off to the side of the road, he handed Anna the reins and hopped down to snap the orange canvas closed.

No sooner had he let down the driver's side covering than the sky opened, and a steady shower bounced off the road as he guided the buggy back to the blacktop. Simon's black standardbred horse threw his head and sidestepped, lurching the cart off the pavement. He led the carriage back to the side of the road and turned on the battery-operated safety lights.

"We best sit tight for a few minutes."

Anna looked at the house less than a quarter of a mile away. "I suppose."

Simon secured the foot brake and relaxed his shoulders against the blue-lined seat. "Thanks for helping *Mamm*. I'm sure you'd much rather be anywhere but here today."

"I like your *mamm*; she was always polite to me."

The only sound in the carriage was the music of the late autumn rain. Showers of colored leaves blew around, leaving a few stuck to the front window. Rex, Simon's horse, dropped his head and let the rain cover his back as Simon and Anna searched for words to fill the void.

Simon wiped his forehead with the back of his hand. "Can I ask you something?"

Anna's eyes fell to the floor. "Do I have a choice?"

"Why did you tell me to go home and live up to my responsibilities?"

Anna articulated, "How hard is it to understand? You have obligations you need to live up to."

"But that's what I'm trying to do."

Anna said, "What makes you think you can do it here in Willow Springs?"

Simon leaned forward and rested his elbows on his knees for a few seconds before responding, "Home is the one place where I have caused the most pain. It was only fitting I return and do my fair share."

Anna tried to think of something to calm the frustration creeping up her neck, but in the end, she spat out, "Whose pain are you talking about? Your pain, my pain, or perhaps your wife's?"

Simon sat up straight. "What on earth are you talking about?"

Anna expressed her frustration with a long sigh and a shake of her head. "I know all about Cora. Last year, she wrote me and clearly told me you wouldn't be coming back to me or your Amish family."

Emptying his lungs of air, he groaned. "Anna, I didn't marry Cora or anyone else for that matter."

Anna stayed quiet for some moments, then spoke hesitantly. "But I thought…"

"You've been misled." Simon turned to face her and continued, "Anna, you must believe me when I say my heart has always belonged to you and no one else." His face flushed, then paled. "I let my guard down with her in a weak moment, and I regret every minute I led her on."

An array of emotions surrounded Anna making it hard for her to speak as she swallowed down her emotions at Simon's statement.

"Anna, I've hurt you, and it will take time to earn your trust back, but won't you please let me try? Don't let the devil have a stronghold of your heart."

Simon saw a spasm of pain cross her face as a single tear trickled down her cheek. He pleaded, "You don't need to answer me now, but promise me you'll think about it." He picked back up the reins.

They rode silently until they pulled into the driveway, and Anna's eyes fixed on the garden. Rain still hung in the air at the passing shower, but the last colorful blooms held their heads to the sky, basking in the last few days of warmth. Fumbling for a handkerchief, Anna wiped her nose, drew a long breath, and said, "I need to pray over it, then leave it in God's hands."

Simon glanced her way and tried to think of something to say that was comforting. "I'll pray that it's His will as well."

***

For the rest of the afternoon, Naomi watched Anna trim back the lavender plants and tie oregano and thyme sprigs to dry over the stove for winter.

"It's a shame you're not somehow putting all your plant knowledge to work for you. Whatever happened to your dream of owning an herb farm?"

"Those dreams are long gone," Anna said wearily.

The older woman bent over to dig the root of an old thistle plant out and threw it in the wheelbarrow. "I would say that's a matter for us to pray over and see where the Spirit leads."

Anna shrugged. "Seems like I'll need the Spirit's direction for many things."

Naomi sat down on a bench at the side of the garden and lifted her chin in the direction of Simon across the yard. "You're not the only one."

Anna followed her gaze for only a second before she busied her hands. She swallowed hard, wondering if she could confide in her old friend. After a long silence, she dropped to her knees and studied the lines around Naomi's eyes.

"What is it, child?"

Finally, she gulped and said, "I thought he was married."

"Who?"

Looking past her to where Simon was splitting wood, Anna said, "Simon."

Naomi's laugh was bigger than life, and when she found her voice, she asked, "What on earth would make you think that?"

"Cora sent me a letter last year telling me so."

Naomi shook her head. "That girl couldn't be trusted. Twisted my boy's better judgment every which way."

Anna tilted her head and flipped her eyes in his direction. "When I received her letter, it was like I had to relive him leaving again."

"Did he set you straight?"

"*Jah.*"

Naomi brushed the dirt off her hands. "Thank the Lord. Maybe now you both can work your way through this misunderstanding."

Anna stood and wiped the mud off the front of her dress. "I'm not so sure it will be that easy."

Simon's mother made a sympathetic clucking noise. She remarked, "Sometimes, we let our head overrule our heart, which will only cause trouble. Don't think too hard about what was but look to the Lord for all answers. He'll never let you down."

The two women sat in thoughtful silence, then Naomi changed the subject.

"Word has it your *datt* is under the weather. Hasn't been to church in over a month."

Anna stopped digging through a deep-rooted weed and leaned on the hoe. "Do you know what the problem is?"

Naomi crumpled her eyebrows together. "*Nee*, can't say I do, but I wanted to mention it."

"I'll tell Matthew and my *schwesters.*" Anna resumed loosening the soil with her hoe and added, "Not too sure what we can do about it. It's not like Wilma would let us help even if *Datt* let us in."

"You could at least try," returned Naomi with loving concern.

"It's been almost two years. I'm certain he won't budge."

Naomi stood. "End of life softens even the most hardened souls. And don't give up on this community yet. I think things are about to change."

Anna gasped, "End of life? Is he that bad? And what do you mean about the community?"

"It must be serious for Jacob Byler to miss two church services. As far as this community goes, you all have stirred things up, and many older ones are starting to question the *Ordnung.*"

The old woman didn't say anything but left Anna alone in the garden. Her chest suddenly heavy with worry, she turned her face to the parting sun and prayed for her father's health.

***

Simon eyed Anna as she held her face to the sun. His biceps tightened as he swung the ax over his head and let it land, splitting the dried oak log in two. He wanted to run to her but set up another log on its end and swung again to keep his desire under control. In the back of his head, a small voice whispered, *Patience, my son.*

As he conversed with his Heavenly Father, he realized all his cares and burdens concerning Anna became just a small part of God's plan. The old Simon, consumed with his own pleasures, would have bolted over to Anna and demanded that she give him an answer. But the new Simon was trying hard to be patient and wait on God to point the way.

CHAPTER 7

It was still dark when the clock made Wilma Byler aware that life still went on in the quiet farmhouse regardless of how long she'd been awake. She took a long look around the kitchen, wishing there was something she could do to take her mind off how worried she was about Jacob.

Climbing the stairs slowly, she stood in the doorway and studied the rise and fall of her husband, Jacob's, chest. The glow from the kerosene lamp on the dresser bounced shadows off the wall in unison with his labored breaths. Laying the back of her hand on his damp forehead, she sighed at the warmth.

Another day with no change, Wilma headed back downstairs with misty eyes. Jacob's stubbornness forbade her to send for the doctor, but she had an unsettled concern about his progress. They needed help, but who could she turn to? Guilt consumed her at the part she played in encouraging Jacob to side with the community and not his children. Was this God's punishment for her selfishness in wanting to keep Jacob all to herself?

Never having children of her own, she was jealous of her new husband's desire to stay connected to his adult children. She understood the last few years had not been easy on any of them but forcing his hand in their ex-communication changed Jacob. He missed his children and mourned the loss of his grandchildren to the point of depression.

The news made him despair as soon as he heard Rebecca was about to have her second child. On more times than she could count, she found him standing on the porch, straining to hear Matthew's young twin daughter's laughter through the trees that separated their farms.

Wilma drew on her hat and coat, picked up the egg basket, and headed to the barn. An early morning wind swirled around her skirt, reminding her winter was close at her heels. How would she ever take care of the animals, the furniture business, and the house all by herself?

Trouble and sorrow rolled over Wilma in such a tidal wave she clutched the barn door and cried out, "Oh, Lord, what have

I done? If you can hear me, Lord, please forgive me for all the wrong I've done to this family."

***

"Rebecca, what should we do? If *Datt* is sick, shouldn't we at least try to see if Wilma needs our help?"

"I can't see either one going against Bishop Weaver's ruling," admitted Rebecca.

Anna refilled their coffee cups and wiped the milk off Mary Ellen's tray before sitting back at the table. "I think I will talk to Emma and Matthew after I tidy up the kitchen. Maybe they've heard something with living so close."

Rebecca balanced John Paul over her shoulder and patted his bottom until his whimpers surpassed. "I'm not sure how much help I'll be, but I'll agree to anything you decide."

Anna stirred cream in her cup. "*Mamm* would expect us to be there for him, especially if he's under the weather."

"But Anna, that was before Wilma came into the picture; that woman is...."

Anna interrupted, "Rebecca, don't go there. Get those ugly thoughts out of your head. Like it or not, the woman is our stepmother and deserves our respect, regardless of how she's treated us."

Rebecca jerked her head to the side and let an unladylike, "Tsk, ugh!" spill from her lips.

"Come on now, I thought we'd seen the last of that snippy attitude from you."

"You have; that woman just gets under my skin!" John Paul stirred with Rebecca's tone. She continued softly, "If it weren't for her, I'm certain *Datt* wouldn't have pushed so hard to have us excommunicated."

"Now, we know nothing for sure. *Datt* was only following the rules of the *g'may*. It was our choice to walk away from the Old Order."

Rebecca stood and swayed, rubbing small circles on her son's back. "I wouldn't change a thing, but it would have been nice for *Datt* to know his grandchildren."

Anna washed Mary Ellen's face and placed her on the floor. "Maybe God already has a plan we don't understand. Naomi seems to think we have cause to hope for this community."

"How so?"

"People are starting to ask questions about the *Ordnung*. Has Eli mentioned anything about that?"

"*Nee.*"

Rebecca laid the baby in the cradle and pulled Mary Ellen onto her lap. "Go ahead and go now. You've been doing so much for me; it's about time I get back to caring for my children and this house myself."

Anna tied her blue headscarf around her chin and slipped into her coat. "I hope to catch Emma at the bakery; maybe she'll go to Matthew's with me."

***

Anna pulled her coat tighter and ducked her chin against the wind. The bitter fall morning left swirls of wood smoke floating along Mystic Mill Road. She would swear it was winter if it weren't for the crimson maple trees. Her nose burned both from the cold and an array of emotions that edged on closing her throat.

Too many things were muddling around in her head; she had trouble deciding which one to pray about first.

Lord, I'm so consumed with everything I'm facing that I don't even know where to start. Please fill me with the Holy Spirit today and give me the wisdom to do the right thing.

Just like I've turned over whatever you have planned for Simon, I also want to turn over this separation from Datt. There are so many hurt feelings, and our family is broken. I can't believe it's what you have in store for us. Please help us find a way to see each other again. And that goes for Simon as well. Is this your will? If so, please make it perfectly clear, and give me the strength to leave it at your feet. Amen.

When Anna stepped off the side of the road to let a truck pass, the black Ford reminded her of Simon and the picture hanging from his rearview mirror. The image of the woman and the child struck her so hard that day at the dry goods store that it took twenty minutes of running before she could think straight.

She thought he was married all this time, and the picture only confirmed it. Getting her emotions back in line would take more than a few days. But even so, it didn't explain the child. If he wasn't married, whose child was Cora holding and why would he carry their picture?

At one time, having children, but more importantly, Simon's children, was all she could think about. Did she dare even let her mind wander about such things? She shook her head, hoping her heart would follow.

A mixture of wood, sugar, and spice wafted through the air as she stepped into Yoder's Bakery.

Katie stood at the counter. "Good morning, Anna. What has you out and about so early?"

"I'm hoping I could speak with Emma if she's not too busy."

"I'm certain she'd enjoy the break. She's been making donuts for hours."

Anna took a cinnamon roll off the tray Katie held out and made her way to the kitchen.

Emma added kindling to the deep fryer wood box and latched the door before turning her way. "Well, hello there, *schwester*. How did you get away from Rebecca's little ones this morning?"

"I had a disturbing talk with Naomi Kauffman yesterday. I needed to see you and Matthew."

"Matthew went to pick up a load of horses from Sugarcreek. He won't be back for a few days. So, all you got is me. What's on your mind?"

"Naomi said *Datt's* been sick. Says he hasn't been to church in three weeks."

Emma dropped a piece of dough in the fryer and watched it sizzle. "Does she say what's the matter?"

"*Nee*. I'm concerned. It's not like *Datt* to miss church."

"I'm not sure what we can do. Wilma will never let us see him."

Emma dropped a few donut rings into the hot oil. "Perhaps we need to put it in God's hands."

Anna sat on a stool near the stainless-steel worktable and picked at her roll. "I think we should at least try. Don't you think *Mamm* would want us to check on him?"

"What did Rebecca say?"

Anna's heart grew anxious. "She left it up to us."

"Anna. I tried to see him about a month ago, and Wilma stopped me at the gate. She didn't say a word but turned her back to me. That pretty much told me all I needed. They are both dead set on abiding by the ruling. Samuel and Matthew have tried talking to him, but nothing."

"What did Matthew and Samuel want to talk to him about?"

"They've been trying to reach out to everyone in the Old Order, especially *Datt*. They're on a mission to spread the Gospel. It's important to them that everyone understands that the way to Jesus doesn't rely on how well they follow the *Ordnung*."

"I can't imagine *Datt* or Wilma ever wanting to leave the old ways."

Emma flipped the donuts. "It's not a matter of leaving the Old Order; it's about following Jesus. All I can do is keep praying for his heart to soften. I can't believe he's content not having his children or grandchildren around. Matthew said he caught him watching the twins through the trees."

Anna's eyes turned sad. "Oh, that breaks my heart. Just the thought of Matthew and Sarah's girls not knowing him hurts. And to think, *Datt* longing for them is so depressing."

"Tell me about it. After everything Samuel and I went through with losing James, not being able to share our news with him is awful. As you said, *Mamm* wouldn't be happy about this."

Anna stood and wiped her sticky fingers on a napkin. "Well, I'm going to try. The worst that can happen is she turns me away. But I will not leave until she tells me what's the matter with him. We have the right to at least know his ailment."

***

Wilma stood in the doorway as Dr. Smithson walked through the gate and up the porch steps. Her eyes were wide with fear as she led the doctor to their room. "I'm afraid for him. I've tried everything, and he's not getting any better."

Dr. Smithson took his coat and hat, laid them over the rocking chair, and opened his bag. "How long has he been like this?"

"He hasn't felt well for weeks, but he's been wheezing like that for three days. Hasn't so much as gotten out of bed in as long."

Using a stethoscope to study Jacob's lungs, he flipped them around his neck and picked up his limp wrist. "Fever and pneumonia," he snorted. "You should have called me earlier."

Wilma pulled a chair up to the side of the bed and watched as he worked on breathing some life back into her husband. After giving her a list of instructions and medicine, he added, "Remember, lots of fluids. And I'd get Anna over here to make some strong herbal tea. She was a big help when her mother was ill, and I'd feel better if she was here to help you."

"It might be better if you tell me what you think he needs; I'm not so sure I can get Anna here."

Dr. Smithson drew on his coat and picked up his bag. "I've been doctoring this Plain community for forty years, and I've never seen anything like it. Fathers against daughters, families being torn apart. This one not talking to that one. Ridiculous! And then Jacob at the head of it. I've always held him in high regard and admired his faith. But this splitting of the community has me baffled."

Wilma shuffled behind him as he headed to the door. After seeing him out, she went back to sit at her husband's side. He still lay breathing hoarsely but sleeping. He stirred slightly but sank back to sleep as the minutes turned into an hour.

After running a pan of water and collecting a few fresh towels, she walked back to his bedside and stared at his flushed face on the pillow. She placed the compresses on his warm forehead and whispered, "Jacob, please forgive me. I'm sorry I forced you to turn your back on your children. This isn't right. I promise I'll find a way to bring your family back together if you fight through this."

Her stomach lurched as his raspy cough forced his chest to heave in labored breaths. His eyes flickered opened but shut once the cough subsided, and she cried out to God. *Please, Lord, show me what I need to do.*

***

The closer Anna got to her father's house, the more her pulse quickened. She pushed a fresh wave of anxiety away as she asked God to help her love Wilma more than she feared her. More than anything, Anna wanted to help her father just like she had her mother. A calm came about as she realized love was stronger than fear, and there was no reason to be frightened. She didn't need to worry if Wilma wouldn't talk to her; she needed to be more concerned about showing her love, and the rest, God would work out if she trusted him. She pulled her shoulders back and knocked on the door.

To her surprise, Wilma opened it. Without saying a word, the two women stood in silence. Years of separation filled the silence as they struggled to fill the void. Lines etched the older woman's face to the point that Anna wondered if the woman was under the weather herself.

In not more than a raspy whisper, Wilma said, "You shouldn't be here."

"Wilma, I'm not here to cause you grief, but I don't care what the bishop or any other community member might say about me being here. I hear my *datt* is ill, and I'd like to see him."

Wilma stuttered, "He…he…isn't good."

"Naomi Kauffman mentioned he hasn't been to church. It must be bad if he can't get out of the house. May I see him?"

Stepping aside, she let Anna enter, and a sudden weakness forced Wilma to the couch. "Dr. Smithson said he has pneumonia."

Without waiting for her stepmother to answer, she headed to the stairs. "Anna?"

"*Jah?*"

"Watch him carefully, and the doctor said you should make him a strong herbal tea."

"Let me check on him first, and then I'll make a Respiratory Tea."

"What do you need to make it?"

"Peppermint, oregano, coneflower, and comfrey leaf. I'm sure *Mamm* had all those things in her garden once."

"I'm not too good with plants, but I think oregano exists. Do you want me to go get some?"

"It might be easier for me to get all I need at once."

Anna barely made it up the stairs before Wilma laid down and pulled a blanket over her shoulders. The woman's dingy *kapp* and soiled dress tugged at Anna's sympathy. For the first time, she had compassion for the woman who took her mother's place in her father's heart.

As the day continued, her father's fever mounted, and he tossed and turned, thrashing in broken sentences. Sometimes he called out to her mother and shouted to his children for others with a mixture of anguish she couldn't always place. When at last his body tired, he drifted off to a restful slumber. Once he settled, Anna massaged Lung Fever Salve over his chest and on the bottom of his feet. Wiping her hands free of cedar oil and menthol, she watched the rise and fall of his chest and prayed.

The hiss of the kerosene lamp over the kitchen table met Anna as she carried a tray to the sink. After a long nap, Wilma moved to the table. "I should have reached out to someone earlier. I'm having a hard time forgiving myself for not doing more."

"But you did, and that's all that matters."

"I had no idea he was so sick. He seemed a little depressed, and we thought he just had a cold. But he didn't bounce back."

After a few minutes of silence, Anna spoke up. "I'm trying to learn to trust God in all of this, but what he needs is family."

Wilma dropped her head, and a tear moved to the end of her nose. Wiping it away with the back of her hand, she verbalized, "I'm to blame for most of that."

Anna tried to console her. "Maybe we can figure it all out when *Datt* gets better." Her stepmother's tears flowed more freely, and she laid her head across her folded arms and mumbled, "I've made so many mistakes."

Anna moved to her side. "Never too many that God won't forgive us for."

Wilma turned her face to look at Anna and asked, "After all I've done to keep you from your father, how can you sound so forgiving?"

"We all go through different challenges in life. Maybe we've been placed in the middle of this so He can shed some light into our hearts."

The older woman sat up, wiped her face with the hem of her black apron, and said, "Your *datt* believes what you and your siblings stand for."

"What? How is that so? He'd been so against us leaving the church."

"It didn't take long for him to realize you were all on to something. After becoming minister, he started studying more, but it was too late by that time."

Anna sat down at the table and leaned in closer. "But Wilma, it's never too late to trust in Jesus."

Wilma's tired eyes filled with tears, and her lips quivered. "It was when he had me chirping in his ear all day to let it be. I just started making friends here and didn't want to leave the Old Order. And besides, I wanted your *datt* all to myself."

Wilma's shoulders shook with sobs, and Anna pulled her close. With a silent prayer for strength, Anna let the shattered woman lean on her as she whispered calming words in her ear.

Her restless form settled, and Anna silently thanked God for allowing her to love the woman who had caused her family so much pain.

"*Denki,* for coming."

"Really, Wilma, it was no trouble. I need to be here taking care of *datt*…and you."

Wilma pulled away and wiped her nose on the crinkled-up hankie she pulled from her sleeve. "Your *datt* is one thing, but me? I don't deserve your kindness."

"Wilma, please, we understand how hard it must have been to step into a ready-made family. Especially when we refused to follow the old ways."

Anna walked to the stove, took the steaming tea kettle to the metal-lined sink, and poured it into a dishpan. Wilma carried a bucket of cold water from the hand pump in the back room and ran just enough in the dishpan to warm the water.

Plopping down in Jacob's place at the table, Wilma sighed. "So many changes to the way things have always been. I'm not sure any older folk want to embrace everything this New Order Fellowship is about."

Anna stopped working on the stack of dirty dishes, dried her hands on a towel, and sat beside her stepmother. "There is only one thing you need to concern yourself with, and that is following what the Bible tells us."

Anna laid her hand across Wilma's arm and said, "Jesus clearly instructs that the only way to the Father is through Him. So that means we must put our trust in Jesus and not a set of rules created by man."

"But what will happen to our heritage and history?" Wilma pleaded.

"Nothing is going to happen to any of that." Anna assured her. "We still keep ourselves separated from the outside world, and we will live the same way. The only thing changing is following Jesus, which means sharing His love with everyone."

"I don't see how Bishop Weaver or any of the other ministers will go for this."

Anna smiled and walked back to the sink. "I don't either, but God is bigger than any of this, and He will find a way to bring this community back together, I'm sure of it."

Wilma's face was pained. "I'm not one to accept change so quickly, but if your *datt* pulls through this, I'll definitely do my part to being open to hearing you children out."

Anna looked over her shoulder. "How about you go sit with *Datt*? I'll finish up these dishes and be up in a minute."

Jacob slept all day, and Wilma did not leave his side. Once, when Anna came up to check on him, Wilma was on her knees by the bedside. The next time she sat quietly, stroking his hand, speaking in hushed tones. There was no doubt in Anna's mind that her stepmother truly cared for her father. She was wrong about her stepmother and silently asked God to forgive her for all the times she let her mind drift to unpleasant thoughts about the woman who took her beloved *mamm's* place.

CHAPTER 8

Jacob rested and slept for a week as Anna and Wilma took turns helping him regain strength. Anna stayed in her old room and reported to her siblings about his care. Even when her father was less than cooperative in her presence, she came into his room with a cheerful greeting.

When she slid a chair close to his bedside and opened the jar of salve, he quickly took the container from her hand. "I'm done with that stinky stuff. And besides, I'm more than capable of rubbing it on my chest."

Anna tugged it back from her father. "You might as well resign yourself to my care until you're up and out of this bed."

She unscrewed the metal lid and held up the jar. "This ointment had a lot to do with your recovery."

121

Jacob swung his feet over the side of the bed and growled, "Why are you here?"

"That's a silly question. Why else would I be here but to take care of you? And besides, I was part of Dr. Smithson's order. Well, me and my Respiratory Tea."

Her father stammered and took a labored breath. "I...I...think it's time for you to leave. Any care I need...Wilma can tend to."

A pang of hurt landed deep in Anna's chest, and she gulped hard before responding. "I was hoping we could bury all this behind us and start fresh."

Jacob steadied himself on the nightstand as he stood. "Are you coming back to the Old Order?"

"*Nee*, I'm not."

"Then we have nothing left to say. I will have to go before the bishop with you being here. Wilma should never have allowed you in."

Anna reached out, and he pulled away as a look of pain passed over his pale face. "Anna, please, you need to go."

She set the jar of salve on the stand, looked her father in the eye, and said, "You can continue to push us away, but we will never turn our backs on Jesus."

Jacob lowered himself back to the bed as soon as his daughter left the room. The desperate crack in her voice tugged at his heart. Once keen and analytical, his mind seemed broken and lethargic, much like his body. He knew her care probably pulled him through the worst of his sickness, and she did have a way with herbs and tonics.

He laid in his bed, listening to the friendly chatter between Wilma and Anna for days. He never thought it possible that the woman would ever warm up to his children. But again, it was Anna; her sweet disposition rubbed off on Wilma, eventually winning her over. He longed to regain his strength and get on with life. But he had one uneasiness that continued to haunt him throughout his ordeal. And that was his first wife's, Stella's, dying wish.

***

The November wind snapped at Anna's head scarf as she tied her horse to the hitching rail beside Shetler's Grocery. Barbara Miller greeted her as she stepped inside and out of the wintry air. Several shoppers in dark brown bonnets and black coats mingled around the store and smiled at her as she entered.

It had been a week since her father turned her away, and her mood had spiraled much like the wind through the gray skies. Anna went to the back of the store where colorful bolts of fabric were stacked neatly between the shelves. Rebecca had sent her for a fabric supply in preparation for the winter sewing season.

She picked out blue chambray for Eli's work shirts and a dark purple and blue royal crepe for new dresses for herself, Mary Ellen, and Rebecca. Blue denim was on the list for little pants for John Paul and work trousers for Eli. Finally, she added a white organdy to her pile for new *kapps*.

Barbara moved to her side, laid the fabric bolts on the long worktable, and asked how much she needed of each. After Anna told her the total yardage, she added black winter stockings, thread, and shirt buttons to the table.

Barbara slipped a couple of straight pins between her lips and mentioned. "You just missed Simon."

Just the mention of his name made her stomach flip. "That's good; I'm in no mood to entertain his questions."

"Are you going to give the man another chance?"

Anna let out a long sigh. "I don't know what I want to do. I'm starting to feel like I'm in the way at Rebecca and Eli's,

Datt refuses to let me help him, and I don't like working in the yarn shop."

"*Stitch n' Time*? I thought that was something you and Rebecca did together."

"*Nee*, that's Rebecca's dream, not mine."

"Do Emma and Katie need help at the bakery?" Barbara asked.

"Even that leaves a sour spot in my stomach. I enjoy making peanut brittle, but do I want to bake every day? I don't think so."

"Sounds like you need a change of scenery."

Anna whined. "As long as that scenery doesn't involve a bunch of people. I'm uncomfortable when I get around lots of faces. I can barely handle waiting on customers at the yarn shop."

Barbara laid her scissors down and walked to the bulletin board at the front of the store, waving Anna to follow her. "An *Englisch* man stopped by this morning and asked if I knew of an Amish woman who would be interested in being a nanny."

She removed the thumbtack and handed Anna the postcard. *NANNY FOR HIRE. Looking for a responsible young woman to care for an eight-month-old baby. Transportation and meals provided. Lake Erie area. Please call for more information.*

"So, what do you think? It might be just what you need to figure out what you want to do about Simon. Some time away."

"But what do I know about babies?"

Barbara laughed before replying. "Anna don't be silly. You've been taking care of Rebecca's children for months now, and if you can calm colicky John Paul down, you can handle an eight-month-old. Besides, you have a way of calming *kinner* down. Who does everyone go to during church when they need a break? You, of course."

"I suppose. But Erie is an hour and a half away. That's a long trip back and forth every day."

Barbara took the postcard back and looked it over again. "I got the impression they wanted someone to care for the child in the house and stay with them during the week. They asked about church services and wanted to be sure it was a single girl who didn't have a family she needed to return to each night."

"My palms are sweating just thinking about it. A strange house and an *Englisch* one at that."

"Oh, come on, Anna. It would be good for you. It will give you time to ponder the future and get away from this church division for a while. God knows I'd like nothing more than to leave Willow Springs for a short time myself."

"You want to leave Willow Springs?"

Barbara looped her arm in Anna's. "*Nee,* not really. But with Joseph back in the picture and two little boys underfoot, a change of scenery certainly sounds tempting."

Anna tucked the card into her black pocketbook and picked up the stack of fabric. "I'll keep the card for a few days and bring it back if I decide not to call."

"Do it. I think it will be good for you. Nothing like a baby to take your mind off your worries."

Barbara leaned in close and whispered, "And besides, I guarantee you Simon Kauffman needs a taste of his own medicine, if you grasp what I mean."

Anna slapped her friend's arm away. "That's not nice. I know how it feels to be left behind, and that's not something to look forward to."

"I'm just kidding, but it wouldn't hurt for Simon to feel what it's like to be left in limbo."

In a severe tone, Anna asked, "But what if I decide I don't want to give him another chance right now? I can't expect him to wait on me forever."

"I'd say that's a conversation you need to have with him. And as antsy as he is to have you back in his life, he's not going to like it one bit."

Anna tilted her head and furrowed her brow. "I'm not sure why he's in such a hurry all of a sudden. I waited on him for years, and once I finally thought I'd closed that part of my heart, he wants me to open it like a window at the first sign of spring."

A customer walked up behind them, and Barbara leaned in close and said, "Take your time. When the time is right, God will direct your path."

***

The following day, after Rebecca had gotten the children down for an afternoon nap, Anna spread out the denim material and retrieved the homemade brown paper patterns from the drawer. Trying not to waste a bit of fabric, Anna carefully cut out enough pieces for two pairs of trousers.

Rebecca pulled a chair to the treadle sewing machine in front of the window to take advantage of the ready-made sunlight. As she lifted the cabinet's lid, elevating the sewing machine head from a concealed position, she asked, "You've been awfully quiet this morning. What's weighing so heavily on your mind?"

Anna stacked the cutout fabric pieces in a neat pile and pushed them to the side of the table. "I suppose I've been pondering a few things this morning."

Rebecca sifted through the drawer until she found the exact color of the thread needed and proceeded to fill a bobbin. "I'm all ears if you'd like to talk things through."

Smoothing out the wrinkles in the blue chambray material, Anna replied, "What would you say if I was thinking about taking a nanny job in Erie for a short time?"

Rebecca placed a filled bobbin beneath the plate under the pressure foot and turned in her chair. "Why would you want to take on a job? You already have one in the yarn shop."

Anna pinned a paper pattern to the material and replied, "That's just it. *Stitch n' Time* is your passion, not mine, and you understand I'm uncomfortable dealing with customers. And besides, I'm starting to feel like you and Eli could use some time without me underfoot so much."

"Now that's just plain crazy. I wouldn't know what to do without you here. You've been such a help to me, especially with the *kinner*."

"I reckon so, but for what it's worth, I need to figure out what I want in life, and right now, my head is going in a million different directions. I think if I allow myself a change of scenery for a time, things will become clearer."

Rebecca put the first piece of fabric under the needle and lowered the pressure foot to keep them in place. With her right hand, she gave a quick tug to the wheel on the side of the machine, and with her foot, she rocked the treadle beneath the machine, setting the needle in motion. "You've never been content in the yarn shop, but becoming a nanny, what do you know about doing that type of work?"

"I assume it won't be much different from what I've been doing for you, except I'll be living with an *Englisch* couple during the week."

Rebecca carefully guided the needle along the seam of Eli's new pants a quarter of an inch from the edge. "You can't even go to the store without breaking out in a cold sweat. How do you think you'll be able to go live with a strange couple in unfamiliar surroundings?"

Anna sighed as she folded the cut fabric pieces in a neat stack. "Rebecca, please understand, I need to get away from Willow Springs for a time. With Simon back, my emotions are all stirred up, and I can't seem to think straight. I'm hoping if I step away for a little bit, God will make things clearer for me."

Snipping the ends of a loose thread, Rebecca asked, "Are you going to tell Simon?"

Anna slipped into a chair, propped her elbows up on the table, and rested her chin in her hands. "Ohhhh...I don't know. Do you think I should?"

The sewing machine stayed quiet for a moment before Rebecca said, "All I can say is you need to remember how you felt when he took off without any word of his plans or where you stood. I don't think you have it in you to do the same to him."

"Maybe you're right. I sure wish *Mamm* were still around. I could use some of her wise words about now."

Rebecca moved to Anna's side and rested her arm on her shoulder. "Perchance, are you trying to figure everything out on your own? What would *Mamm* say to you right now?"

Anna rested her forehead in her palms and muttered, "She would say I need to get out of God's way and quit trying to pick up his pen. He'll write the words himself and doesn't need my help."

"Precisely. Now, if you feel strongly about this nanny job, I'd say you need to discuss it with God. Perhaps he's laid it in your path for a reason."

Anna reached up and patted her *schwester's* hand. "How have you become so smart about things?"

"Smart, absolutely not, but I've learned from my past mistakes. It never turns out well when I get in God's way or think I know better than him."

"But what if that's not what He has planned for me? Could it be I'm just running away from Simon because I don't like the conflict it's causing me to face?"

Pulling out a chair beside her, Rebecca answered, "Whenever I'm struggling with a decision, I go back to the questions Bishop Weaver explained to us once. First, does what I want to do line up with scripture? Second, have I researched and fully understand the consequences of my decision? And lastly, have I sought wise counsel?"

Anna sat up straight. "I'd forgotten about that sermon. Thanks for reminding me. I'll do those things before I make my final decision."

Rebecca stood and headed toward the back bedroom. "Do you mind finishing that pair of pants while I care for John Paul?"

Anna nodded and took a seat at the sewing machine. The constant motion of the needle and the pedaling with her foot calmed her anxiety. At least she was able to line her thoughts up in order. After supper, she would call the number on the card to ask more questions about the job. Next, she would spend the evening searching scripture for guidance, and then she would think of someone else she could talk to that would give her direction.

Perhaps Bishop Schrock, better yet, maybe she could have a heart-to-heart with Naomi. Even if she was Simon's mother, she could always count on the older woman to speak truth into a situation.

***

As soon as Anna finished helping Rebecca with the supper dishes, she settled down at the kitchen table with a pen and paper. The thought of facing Simon was too much; a letter would have to do.

Eli quietly read Mary Ellen a story, and Rebecca was nursing the baby in the living room. An early November cold front left everyone wanting to stay close to the wood stove that nicely warmed the two rooms separated by a wide doorway.

Anna looked up from her letter and glanced around the room. The cozy scene left her yearning for a family of her own, which only made the words she needed to write even more challenging.

Watching Eli and Rebecca sitting in their matching willow-bent rockers beneath the glow of the gaslight tugged at her heart. The baby cooed softly as Rebecca placed him over her shoulder. Eli winked at her *schwester* in the most endearing manner, making Anna turn away before her brother-in-law caught her staring.

She added a few words to the lined paper, only to tear the sheet from the notebook and wad it up in a ball. Giving up on the letter, she opened her Bible and let the pages fall as they may, leaving James 2:4 before her. '*Ye have not because ye ask not.*'

Re-reading the verse a few times, she asked, "Eli, what do you think this verse from James 2:4 means? '*Ye have not because ye ask not.*'"

Eli set Mary Ellen on the floor and picked up his Bible to turn to the book of James. After reading the scripture for himself, he stopped to think before answering. "I think we need to read verses one through three to get James's entire message. He is trying to get us to see the motives behind what we ask for. Reading it closely reveals that the problem is not really in the asking. The problem is in the reason why you are asking."

"I guess I'm still not understanding it."

Eli carried his Bible to the table and sat down beside her. "What drives many of us is the burning desire to get something we don't have. This is known as coveting. To be jealous of something someone else has, or to possess an eagerness to get something that doesn't belong to us."

Anna traced her finger over the scripture again and asked, "How do I know if I'm doing this?"

Eli looked at her tenderly and asked, "How do you feel when you see others around you being blessed and it seems like God is passing you by? Do you rejoice in their blessing, or do you envy them?"

Anna sat quietly, recalling her yearning when watching her *schwester's* family.

Eli continued, "Look at James 2:3 again. '*When you ask, you do not receive, because you ask with wrong motives, that you may spend what you get on your pleasures.'*"

Reaching for a cookie out of the covered plastic dish in the center of the table, Eli said, "God chooses not to answer prayers pursued with wrong motives. Can you imagine how we would be if God answered our prayers from our selfish motives? We'd all be a big mess."

Eli reached for another cookie and headed back to the living room. Anna studied the verses again and couldn't help but question her own motives. Was she asking for God to set her path straight for selfish reasons? Why was she so eager to run away from Simon?

In her heart, it was easy to answer her own questions. She wanted Simon to suffer as she had. And yes, she wanted to leave Willow Springs because watching Rebecca and Emma and their perfect families made her jealous.

She was even more confused now. She didn't want to pray for clarity if it meant she was hiding behind her own selfish desires. Was the fear of being hurt again forcing her to run away from what her heart truly wanted?

To walk away from anyone or anything that would cause her distress in hopes she could keep her anxiety tied up in a neat little box. Hadn't she done that her whole life? Stay safe, at arm's length, not letting anyone upset the balance of her life.

That was until Simon came along. He was the only one she let in and look what he did. He'd emptied the whole apple cart at her feet, spilling an array of emotions she tried so hard to keep neat and tidy.

Anna rested her folded hands on her closed Bible and prayed.

Lord, please make your desires my desires. I'm not sure what you want me to do, but I have faith you will guide my steps along the way you want me to travel. If it's Simon, show me your will. If you want me to care for that little one, clear the path and make it happen. And please remove the envy from my heart and help me celebrate alongside Rebecca and Emma's blessings. I know my day is coming; I'm sure of it. Just help me be patient while waiting. Most of all, help me remember that asking and faith matter greatly, but my motives matter more. Amen.

She carried her cup to the sink and told Rebecca she was heading to make a call. She wrapped a shawl around her shoulders before heading out the door. Once inside the phone shanty, she turned on the battery-operated lantern and retrieved the postcard from her pocket.

Her heart raced as she dialed the number. On the third ring, a man answered, "Buckhannon residence."

CHAPTER 9

All morning, Anna played her conversation with Mr. Buckhannon in her head. A *bobbli* cried in the background as she asked him to explain what the nanny job consisted of. His major concern was that whoever they hired was able to stay with the child throughout the week. The baby needed a daily companion and caretaker. Mr. Buckhannon declared he and his wife would care for the child over the weekend, leaving her to return home for a couple of days.

He mentioned he'd like to set up a live interview and a chance to meet the child beforehand if she was interested. Her usual uneasiness when making a phone call, especially to a stranger, was gone, replaced with an overwhelming peace.

After she hung up, she couldn't help but notice how confident she felt about accepting the position. But she refused to commit to anything before she had a chance to talk with Naomi or Bishop Schrock.

As she unlocked the door to the yarn shop, she heard the clip-clop of an approaching buggy and stopped to welcome their visitor. God himself had already set her day in motion, and she smiled at His goodness when she bid good morning to Naomi.

Walking back down the steps, she held her hand out to help the older woman down from her enclosed buggy. Without asking, she picked up the lead off the buggy floor, fastened it to Naomi's horse's bridle, and wrapped it around the hitching post.

"What has you out and about on this chilly morning?"

Naomi loosened the ties on her heavy brown bonnet and followed Anna back up the stairs. "I needed a few things at the Mercantile, and for some reason, I felt led to stop by and check on you."

Anna only smiled as she pushed open the door, took the lamp from the center of the worktable, and jiggled it slightly to hear if there was enough fuel in the tank. "I'm glad you did. I would like to talk to you about something."

Naomi held her hands over the small wood stove in the corner of the room. "Jebediah said the cow's neck hair is extra thick this year. That's a sure sign we are in for a hard winter. Even the Farmer's Almanac is predicting it."

Anna nodded in agreement. "I'm thankful Eli came out early and lit the stove for me. This cold spell came early, for sure and certain."

Anna put the lamp on the table, attached a small pump to the valve on the base, and pumped a dozen or so strokes before turning the nob to allow a small amount of fuel in the narrow tube. With a quick light from two matches, the flame ignited, and she adjusted the light and hung it on a hook from the ceiling.

Anna held her hand to the side of the teapot on the stove. "I made a pot of lemon verbena tea this morning. It should have seeped long enough by now. Would you like a cup?"

"Just what I need to warm these old bones."

Anna took two mugs below the counter and a honey pot and set them in front of her.

Naomi held her cup up for Anna to fill. "So, what did you want to talk to me about?"

After stirring a healthy spoon of honey into her cup, Anna turned serious. "You've been a dear friend to me over the years, especially since my mother died."

After a thoughtful pause, Anna went on. "I don't want to put you in the middle of the challenges I'm having with accepting Simon's return."

Naomi looked dubious. "Why do I think there is a but coming?"

"Not really. I just need some sound advice, and I trust your opinion."

Naomi took a long sip of her tea. "What is it, child?"

Anna signed. "I'm thinking of taking a nanny job in Erie."

"Oh, my dear! What brought this on?"

"I'm confused and think I need a change of scenery."

"I understand Simon's return caught you off guard. But are you sure you're not just running away?"

Anna sipped her tea and took a few seconds before replying. "I asked myself that same question. And I keep going back to trusting in God to lead me where he wants me to go. At this moment, I felt led to answer the ad for a nanny."

"How about you tell me a little about the job?"

"I spoke to the couple last night. Seems the child is quite a handful for the older couple, and they need help tending to his daily needs. It would only be during the week, and I can return home on the weekends. They will send a weekly driver to fetch me late Sunday evening and take me home early Saturday morning."

Naomi tightened her grip on her mug and tried not to let Anna know her concerns. Somehow, she had to convince the girl to stay in Willow Springs. Little did Anna know that Simon was counting on her to help him bring his son home. In the back of Naomi's head, she was contemplating how Simon would still get to see her, and it might be enough time each week to regain her trust.

Pausing long enough to send up a quick prayer for the right words, Naomi stated, "Caring for a baby is hard work, let alone becoming attached to a child whom you may never see again. Are you up for that?"

"I haven't thought of that, but the assignment is only for a few months until the woman gets back on her feet. Seems she's been under the weather and hasn't been able to give the child the care he needs."

"Are you sure you're not taking this job just so you don't have to face what the future might bring?"

"Oh, Naomi, my head is swirling with so many things, and I can't help but think if I leave here for a little bit, I'll see God's plan play out better."

"What is it you want clarity on?"

Anna set her cup down, folded her hands, propped up her elbows on the work counter, and rested her chin on her fingers. "Like why God isn't delivering me from my fears."

Naomi made a little sympathetic clucking noise and remarked, "The main reason we suffer is because God isn't so concerned with our comfort or happiness in this life."

"What do you mean?" Anna asked, surprised.

"His goal is our eternal happiness. When He allows for difficulties in this life, it's because He's more interested in building our faith, changing our character, and freeing us from our fears here on earth."

Releasing a long breath from her lungs, Anna asked, "Are you saying I'll always be fearful of the future and making the wrong decision?"

"Not necessarily; I am saying He may allow it to happen so you will draw closer to Him. If you didn't struggle with fear and anxiety, you wouldn't have any need for Him."

"But Rebecca and Emma, or any other girl my age, doesn't seem to suffer like I do. Why aren't they bothered by such things?"

Naomi looked amazed. Then laughed lightly. "Is your memory so short you don't remember Emma questioning her faith? What about Rebecca? Didn't she struggle with pride and a sharp tongue? Just because they don't struggle the same as you, doesn't mean their challenges weren't meant to draw them closer to the Lord."

Anna let out a long breath. "So, do you think taking this job is good or not?"

After a few seconds of deep thought on how she could advise her young friend, Naomi decided that God was bigger than anything she or Simon could do. She needed to leave it to Him. "I can't tell you that. Only God can point you in that direction. But I think He is interested in seeing a change in you. And who knows? He may have orchestrated this job for a reason. He may be glorified because of it, which is the goal of everything He does."

Anna quietly said, "I feel like God is directing me to take it. I have peace about it like nothing I have ever done before."

"Well, I can't argue with that. If you and the Lord agree on something, that is all the reassurance I need."

"*Denki*, Naomi. And I appreciate you taking the time to talk to me, even if you shouldn't be here."

"Like I said before, you let Jebediah and I worry about such things. This whole church split thing is for the birds in my books. The more Jebediah and I learn, the more we think you younger folks have it right. I wouldn't be surprised if you don't see the likes of these old folks showing up to your church before too long."

Anna reached for Naomi's hand and squeezed. "You really think so?"

"I'm sure the situation will right itself in time."

"I wish my *datt* would see things that way. Wilma let me in to help, but he sent me away once he got some of his strength back."

Naomi looked dubious. "Don't let that get you down. I think he's already been thinking long and hard about what those manmade rules have cost him. Change is coming. I feel it in my bones."

"You're such a comfort, Naomi. *Denki* again."

"We must pray that God will deal with our leaders and stir their hearts to a point they want nothing better than to follow Christ. I know my Jebediah's heart has been changin'. And I suspect old Bishop Weaver and your *datt* will be following suit anytime now."

Anna clapped her hands under her chin. "I hope you're right. I would love nothing more than to see my family reunited."

"Tell your *schwesters* and *bruder* not to give up hope and don't stop praying for a change. I'm sure God is using this to help us all. Sometimes He uses sharp tools to shape our lives, and I believe he is using this to prepare us for a special purpose."

Then silence reigned, broken only by a log falling in the woodstove. Naomi tied her bonnet in place and headed to the door. "I must go but promise me one thing first."

"What's that?"

"Talk to Simon before you leave."

Anna didn't answer but nodded in the woman's direction. The mere thought of facing Simon brought a sick feeling to her stomach. A part of her wanted to leave without saying a word, but her heart told her otherwise. There was no denying his return affected her in ways she didn't think were ever possible again. But was she ready to allow him to bury his heart with hers again? She wasn't too sure of that.

Slipping her arms in her coat, she went to the phone shanty to set up a meeting with Mr. Buckhannon.

***

The chilly ride to the Mercantile gave Naomi ample time to petition God on Simon's behalf. She almost felt guilty for encouraging Anna to take the nanny position. She couldn't deny Anna's peace about stepping out of her comfort zone. As long as she knew the girl, not once had she taken the initiative to do something as bold as taking a job so far away from home.

Perhaps God had a reason for putting the opportunity in front of her. Naomi's only concern was how Simon was going to handle the news. His heart was set on marrying only one girl, Anna. And as he acknowledged last night, she was the only choice he would accept as the mother of his child.

She wondered if her son's faith was strong enough to withstand a *"nee"* from God. Some of our best plans didn't always align with God's purpose, no matter how hard we prayed.

Naomi pulled her buggy aside from the hitching post in the back of the Mercantile and took a long breath as Bishop Weaver pulled up beside her. His stern face and demeanor warned her that it wasn't a day for a friendly hello. As close as he was to pulling in behind her gave her the impression it was his buggy she pulled out in front of as she was leaving *Stitch n' Time*.

***

Anna pushed the door open with some apprehension, now that she had put off speaking to Simon until the last minute; Mast Lumber Mill, the black letters on the door said.

Sarah, her *bruder* Matthew's wife, sat at the front desk and held up a finger while she completed taking an order over the phone. Putting the phone back in its cradle, she asked, "Anna, what has you out and about today? Does Eli need us to deliver more fence posts?"

Anna shifted from one foot to the other. "*Nee*, I...I hoped I could catch Simon on his lunch break and speak to him for a few minutes."

Sarah looked up at the clock the minute the lunch whistle blew loud enough the workers could hear it over the debarker. "Just in time. Go ahead and cut through *Datt's* office; he won't mind. You should find them all gathering in the lunchroom."

Anna hesitated and asked, "Do you mind getting him for me? I'd like to talk to him in private."

Her *schwester-in-law* rose and smiled in Anna's direction. "No problem. You can stay right here. I need to discuss an order with my *datt* anyways."

Anna untied her blue scarf and let it drop around her shoulders. The oil stove in the corner kept the small office plenty warm, which added to the already rising heat from her chest. She agonized over talking with Simon all morning. As she turned from the window, a shadow lingered in the doorway, and she grimaced when his eyes met hers. "Anna?"

Her heart pounded against her chest as she drew in a breath. Simon waited as she wrung her hands together, and while she struggled to find her words, he asked, "Is everything all right?"

"*Jah*, I have something I need to tell you."

Simon took off his straw hat, sending curls of wood shavings to the floor. He pointed to the two chairs under the window. Anna sat, folded her hands in her lap, and looked straight ahead, trying not to make eye contact. She couldn't bear to see the disappointment on his face. "I came to tell you I'm taking a job in Erie."

Simon balanced his elbows on his knees and twirled his hat in his fingers, keeping his eyes focused on the floor. "I see."

Dismay spread over Simon's face. "Tell me about it," he said softly.

"It's a nanny job. The couple is having trouble caring for their baby. Seems the woman has been under the weather lately and has not been able to give the child the attention he needs."

"I thought you were helping Rebecca with her *kinner*. And what about the yarn shop? Doesn't Rebecca need your help with that?"

"Rebecca doesn't need my help any longer, and I don't particularly like working there."

At length, he paused. "Why now?"

"I don't feel I have anything holding me back right now."

"I...thought..." he stammered, at a loss for words.

"I know what you thought," Anna said quietly, "but what you want from me right now, I'm not too sure I'm ready to give."

Simon stood and went slowly to the window on the room's other side while Anna waited listlessly. Pain edged its way over her forehead, and her hands were moist. She wished she could alleviate his pain, but there was no way around it. She needed this time away.

Turning back and making his way to her side, he knelt and picked up her hands in his. "I wish you wouldn't leave. I was hoping we could spend some time together to get to know one another again."

Anna lifted her chin and stared into his eyes. "A few years ago, I would have given anything to hear those words. But right now, they mingle together with a slew of broken promises."

"How am I ever going to make this up to you?"

"Time...Simon, I need time."

He pulled her hands up and rested his forehead on their combined fingers. "Time is not one thing I have much of."

Anna pulled her hands away. "What does that mean? We have our whole life ahead of us. All I want is to be sure of things, and right now, my emotions are all mixed up."

Simon lifted his head with wonder. "So, does that mean there might be hope for us at some point?"

"Simon," her fingers gripped the edge of the chair. "I won't promise anything. All I know right this minute is I felt led to take the job. It's only during the week, and I'll be home on the weekends. If God has it in His plan to help us work things out, I will be open to His promptings. However, now I have peace about taking care of this child. I have no idea what may or may not happen."

Calmly, Simon spoke. "I can't stop you, and I agree that it will happen if it's in God's will. I've already put our future in His hands."

She stood and tied her scarf under her chin. "I must go. A driver is due within the hour."

Simon stood anxiously and asked, "Do you know how long the job is supposed to last?"

"I assume just until the woman gets back on her feet. Three or four months, I think."

A lump formed in the back of Simon's throat, and he swallowed hard as she left. He only had a few months to prove to Cora's parents that he could provide a stable home for Marcus. He wasn't sure they would ever agree to give him custody without Anna. He followed her small form disappear down Mystic Mill Road until his eyes couldn't find a trace of her black coat and blue scarf.

CHAPTER 10

The long black car stopped in front of a spacious two-story old Victorian on the banks of Lake Erie. "Here's your stop, miss," said the driver, then went back to open the trunk to retrieve her small black suitcase.

As the car pulled away, Anna took a long look at the house as the wind blew off the lake, swirling under her skirt. Pushing back down the hem of her dress, she tucked her chin and made her way to the porch. Lights from the front window shone brightly across a light layer of snow that had settled on the stone-lined porch.

Setting her suitcase beside the door, she rang the bell. The chime made an incredible noise, and she couldn't help but smile at the welcoming sound. Hearing footsteps approaching, she straightened her dress and tried to calm the nerves that were set on drying her mouth.

When the door opened, Mr. Buckhannon greeted her. "Anna, you made it. We've been expecting you all afternoon. Please come in out of the cold."

Anna stomped the snow from her boots before stepping in on the tile lined entryway. "The driver got stuck in some traffic on 79."

He held his hand to take her suitcase. "The Mrs. and I have been watching the weather. We are due for a nor'easter off the lake. Supposed to drop over a foot of snow. Haven't seen a forecast like that this early in over forty years."

From her interview with Mr. Buckhannon earlier in the week, she already knew he was a friendly kind of fellow, which she didn't mind since she wasn't much of a talker.

Mr. Buckhannon set her suitcase on the stairs' bottom step and waved for her to follow him. He led the way into a warm and comfortable-looking living room. Mrs. Buckhannon was covered with a blanket in front of the fire and pointed to the chair beside her. "Sit there, close to the fire, and get warm."

As she spoke, she slipped her arms out of her coat and removed her heavy brown bonnet.

Mr. Buckhannon spoke up. "We have your room ready right next to Steven's. The little guy just went to sleep, but I guarantee you it won't last long."

Anna laid her winter things over her lap and looked toward the staircase. "Perhaps I should get settled before he wakes?"

"Now, just relax, Anna. You'll have plenty to do with that little one. I'm afraid we spoiled him greatly, and you'll have your hands full."

Anna shyly reacted. "I hardly think a child can be spoiled, especially at eight months old."

Mr. Buckhannon snorted. "Oh, are you in for a surprise. The boy is quite colicky and hasn't grown out of it yet. I've done my best, which isn't much considering I've held and rocked him for the better part of the last eight weeks since Margaret's back has been giving her fits."

Mrs. Buckhannon asserted, "I've not been able to get him on any schedule, and he's prone to throwing tantrums now." The woman's face twisted in pain as she repositioned herself in her chair. "The pediatrician says he's underweight and isn't thriving, which I don't understand; he eats all the time. Well, I take that back; he always takes a bottle, but he spits most of it back up."

Anna was already concocting a baby tummy calm tincture in her head as she listened to them explain Steven's behavior.

The baby bellowed from his upstairs room as if on cue to prove his demanding nature. Anna stood. "I'd say my job begins."

"Here, let me show you the way," Mr. Buckhannon suggested. "No, no, you stay. I won't have any trouble finding him."

Mr. Buckhannon lifted his hands and smiled. "Be my guest, and good luck."

Anna grabbed her suitcase with a bounce in her step and ran up the stairs. After depositing her bag in the room to the left of Steven's, she quietly pushed the door open and followed the dimly lit nightlight to the boy's crib.

"Now, now, little one." She said in hushed tones. "What's all the fuss about?"

The child was howling so hard it just about broke Anna's heart. Mrs. Buckhannon was right. The infant was skinny and sick looking. His little red face shook in unison as he pulled his knees to his chest.

Anna cradled the small child in her arms and rubbed small circles on his tummy. "Are you having tummy issues, little one?

We'll take care of that as soon as I can. But let's get to know one another first. How about we start with that wet diaper? Then we can see what we can do about that upset tummy."

After changing and dressing him in a fresh sleeper, she carried him downstairs. His cries settled to a whimper when she brought him to the living room. "Mr. Buckhannon, do you mind showing me to the kitchen where I can find his formula?"

He waved her to follow him, but Anna stopped him to ask Mrs. Buckhannon a few questions. "Do you mind if I try a few things on the little guy?"

"What do you mean?"

"I see he has a bit of diaper rash. Sometimes a little bit of plain yogurt will clear that up. And I see he has some cradle cap. If you have some olive oil, that might do the trick in a few days."

Both Buckhannons smiled, and Margaret answered, "You do whatever you see fit. We've tried so many things, it can't hurt for some good old-fashioned baby remedies to add to the mix."

The vote of confidence encouraged Anna, and she bounced Steven over her shoulder as she followed Mr. Buckhannon to the kitchen.

He opened the pantry and pointed to the shelf where the formula was stored. "We've tried a few different kinds. His doctor suggested we try a goat's milk-based formula yesterday. I picked some up this afternoon. Perhaps you should give that a try."

Anna picked up the can and read the directions. "I think we should. He was pulling his knees to his chest when I picked him up like his tummy was upset."

"Would you like me to take him while you mix it up?"

"I think I can handle both. I'm pretty good at juggling things. I've cared for my sister's children for the last few months, so I've gotten pretty good at doing things with one hand."

"All right then. I'm going to my study to get some work done. Make yourself at home, and you know where to find me if you need anything."

Anna rubbed her chin on the top of Steven's head, trying to calm the child while she hurried to get his bottle made. She learned quickly with John Paul, who had a few bouts of colic, that fussy *bobblis* responded better to a quiet person. Her *schwester*, typically high-strung, often took advantage of

Anna's calming personality to tend to John Paul during his moments of distress.

For the rest of the evening, Anna held and rocked Steven in his room, singing in his ear and letting them get to know one another. When he finally drifted off to sleep, she placed him in his crib and made her way to her room.

After unpacking her suitcase and taking advantage of the bright light the lamp on the nightstand gave, she reached for the stack of books she'd brought with her. One on all-natural herb remedies, one on overcoming fear and anxiety, and her leather-bound bible. An overwhelming peace settled somewhere between her heart and her head when she realized, for once in her life, she felt useful.

Steven had taken to her quite nicely, and the way Mr. & Mrs. Buckhannon welcomed her into their home was refreshing. With a sudden urge to write Rebecca, she picked up the flower-lined stationery she'd brought and flicked on the light on the small writing desk under the window.

Dear Rebecca,

My trip to the Buckhannons went as well as expected, considering an accident on 79 delayed us. I was welcomed warmly and given complete control over Master Steven. Mrs. Buckhannon is recovering from back surgery and spent most of the afternoon in the front room in front of a warming fire.

Little Steven has a set of lungs that, even on John Paul's crankiest day, would overpower him. He seems underweight compared to children his age. I think even John Paul will outweigh him within a month or so.

What has me the most concerned is the extent of his temper tantrums when he is not tended to quickly.

Even though this is only my first day here, I am confident this is where God led me. I feel so comfortable here. My room is beautiful and suitable next to Steven's. I even have a door connecting the two, which I have opened just a crack, so I can hear him stir in the middle of the night. I can't wait until morning to see the view from my window. This part of the house overlooks Lake Erie, and I'm sure the scene will be breathtaking.

I'm not so sure I'll be coming home this weekend. A storm is predicted to hit, and I'd hate to have the driver fight the interstate in such weather.

I pretty much wanted to let you know all is well. I should lie down and try to get some sleep if I can. The presence of a

sleeping baby in the next room does something to me, but don't worry, I am really enjoying all of this.
More later, all my love,
Anna

Tiptoeing into Steven's room, Anna brushed her fingertip over the boy's cheek and whispered a sweet goodnight. "I'm not sure what God has in store for us, little one, but I'm here to help you thrive. Maybe God sent me here so we can help each other."

***

Jebediah Kauffman was a man of few words, but when he did speak, his wife and boys stopped to take notice. "Naomi, I'd like you to gather the boys this evening for a family meeting."

Naomi moved the cast-iron skillet, sizzling with bacon, off the fire and turned toward her husband. "All of them? It might be hard to corral everyone up in one place. Most of the grandchildren will need to get to bed for school tomorrow. Let alone the boys' other jobs off the farm."

With a glint in his eye, he smiled. "If anyone can, you'll make it happen."

"May I ask what's so important?"

Jebediah laid his hand on his open Bible. "I've made a decision that will affect us all."

Naomi moved the crisp bacon to a plate and set it on the table. She didn't need to ask what he was referring to; it was the one thing she'd been praying for, for nearly two years. With a shimmer of moisture in her eyes, she asked, "It's time?"

"*Jah.*"

For nearly forty years, her husband only decided on something after much thought and prayer. She didn't need for him to discuss things with her in detail because she was sure he had already hashed it out with the only one who mattered, *God.*

Jebediah held his cup up for her to fill with coffee. "After breakfast, I'm going to meet with Mose Weaver and Jacob Byler."

Naomi filled her cup and asked, "You've been friends since you were all youngsters. They'll try to talk you out of it. You know this, right?"

"*Jah.* That's why I want to meet with the boys. This will affect us all."

After drizzling a spoon of bacon grease in a clean pan, Naomi cracked a couple of fresh eggs and quickly lapped the hot fat over the whites. "Won't be any trouble for Simon and Benjamin; not too sure about the other five."

"It will be up to the older boys to decide what's best for their families, but I feel it's my place to take a stand for what is right according to God's Word."

Naomi filled Jebediah's plate and took a seat to his right. As they both bowed in silent prayer, Naomi thanked God for shining His truth on her husband's heart.

***

Simon sat on a fallen log overlooking the allotment of land his father deeded to him. The three hundred acres his father had purchased fifty years ago were divided between him and his six brothers. His older brothers had all claimed their portion, and only he and his younger *bruder* Benjamin had yet to take their share.

Willow Creek weaved its way along the backside of all seven parcels of prime farmland. At one point, Simon could have cared less about the property. Still, now with Marcus in the picture, he couldn't imagine raising his son anywhere else. A twinge of panic twisted his stomach, and he chased it away as quickly as it entered. He wouldn't give into worry, especially since he had already placed it in God's hand.

With a sketch pad on his lap, he traced out the lay of the land, positioning the gardens and greenhouse at the right angle of the rise and fall of the sun. He didn't give up hope for Anna's dream and made concessions for the herb farm in his plans. He prayed expectantly that God would bring them back together, in His time and at His will.

Sprigs of dried wheat swayed in the breeze as Simon studied a pair of yearlings maneuvering their way through the open field. Oblivious to his presence, the deer meandered into the woods. Memories of the first day of deer season came to mind, and he couldn't help but smile at the possibility of sharing the same with his son someday.

A twig broke, and Simon turned toward the sound. "*Mamm,* what are you doing up here?"

"I saw you head this way and figured it would do me good to take a walk. It's been years since I've been back here."

Simon moved over on the log and held his hand out to help his mother take a seat.

"Whatcha' got there?" she asked.

Simon held his plans up for her to see and pointed to the area beside the woods. "I think the house would be best there. The trees would shield the hot afternoon sun but allow the morning light to warm the porch nicely."

Naomi giggled. "If I didn't know better, I'd say you have a woman's comfort in mind."

"Not just any woman."

"There's no mistaking who that might be."

"Anna stopped and saw me the other day at the sawmill."

Naomi took the pad from his hands and examined the plans he sketched. "*Jah*, and how did that go?"

"She came to tell me she was taking a job in Erie for a few months."

"*Jah*."

Simon furrowed his eyebrows. "You already knew?"

"*Jah*."

"And you weren't going to tell me?"

"It wasn't my news to tell."

"Why didn't you try to stop her?"

"Again, that's between her and God. She felt led to go."

Simon rested his elbows on his knees. "I'm running out of time. My hearing date is only two months from now, and I'm not one step closer to proving I'm capable of caring for Marcus."

Naomi laid her hand on her son's arm. "Simon, quit trying to rush God. He doesn't expect you to sit back and do nothing. He wants you to actively work toward a goal, but He will line things up in His own time. Continue to work on the house and work hard for your *datt* and Mr. Mast."

Simon interrupted, "But I've wasted so much time chasing dreams…."

"And had you not chased those dreams, there would be no Marcus to worry over."

"But I would have had Anna."

"Did you ever think that perhaps God placed you on that path so there would be a Marcus?"

"Why can't I have both?"

"Nobody said you couldn't, but it might not be how you envision."

Simon took his pad back and sat up straight. "For now, my plans include both."

Naomi stood. "I came up here to tell you *datt* is calling a family meeting. I've sent word to all your *bruders* to come by after supper. Not sure where Benjamin is. But I'll catch him when he comes home for afternoon milking."

Simon knew his younger *bruder* was probably hanging out around the Apple Blossom Inn, hoping to catch Bella Schrock's eye. He'd only recently met the young Amish girl from Indiana that had his brother thinking of nothing else. He wasn't too sure the likes of even his *bruder* could convince the girl to give up her *Englisch* notion and step back into the life of the Amish. But again, who was he to judge? He'd done the exact thing, to the extent of losing the one he valued most for his own selfish desires.

Concentrating back on his drawing, he tucked Anna to the side and did an internal count of how many days before he could see her again at church.

***

Jebediah pulled his buggy alongside Bishop Weaver's, retrieved a lead, and fastened his horse to the hitching post in front of Jacob Byler's furniture shop.

The two men sat on the front porch in matching bentwood rockers. Jacob, much thinner than the last time he'd seen him, and Mose wearing his typical stern expression, greeted him as he made his way up the steps. Tipping his hat in their direction, Jebediah addressed them. "Pleasant weather for the second week in November, *jah*?"

Jacob nodded his head in the direction of the pond across the road. "Ducks and geese are already gone. Sign of a hard winter for sure and certain."

Mose grunted. "Saw two woodpeckers sharing a tree. That's another sign."

After a long silence, Jebediah turned and leaned up against the railing. "We've seen things change in our community over the last fifty years, *jah*?"

Jacob replied, "Some good and some bad, I'd say."

Mose bounced his thumbs on the arms of his rocker. "Been times when I've questioned why the good Lord appointed me to this position. That's for sure."

All three men thought in silence for a few minutes.

Jebediah folded his arms across his chest. "In all the years we've been friends, I can't say we've seen eye to eye on everything."

"Nope, can't say we have," Jacob mumbled.

"But there's one thing we all can agree on."

"What's that?" Mose asked.

"We all want to live by the truth," Jebediah replied.

Jacob looked toward Mose, landed on Jebediah, and asked, "What truth is that?"

"You know as well as I do what truth I'm talking about."

Mose held his hand up. "Not you too!"

Jebediah stood, dropping his hands to his side. "I've been studying, and I believe that the young men of the New Order Fellowship are on to something."

Jacob sat quietly, pondering his misgivings about siding with the older Bishop. Being laid up in bed for the last two months gave him ample time to do his own research and come to his own conclusions. None of them corresponded to his Old Order's rules and regulations. At the heart of it, and after wondering if his days on earth were numbered, he sought the truth himself, hoping it would rectify the state of his family.

After letting Mose settle, Jacob added, "I have to admit, I've been questioning the *Ordnung* myself. Change is bound to happen, no matter how pig-headed and driven by tradition we are. God gave us the New Testament to free us from the bondage of the old ways. Isn't that true, Mose?"

Mose raised his voice an octave. "Regardless, you and I accepted our positions to lead this community. What the New Order Fellowship is preaching goes against everything we stand for."

Jebediah relaxed back on the railing. "Isn't following Jesus and loving our neighbor as we love ourselves the only thing God asked us to do?"

Jacob stopped his chair from rocking and leaned his elbows on his knees. "Now that I know the truth, how can I teach my grandchildren the only way to heaven is by how well they follow the *Ordnung*? Thank God all my children chose to leave the Old Order."

Mose directed Jacob. "Now you too! We need to be in obedience to keep the world out. If not, our culture will fade from existence, and there will be no more separation."

"Mose, I don't know all the answers, but I have to believe God has a new focus for all of us."

"What's that?" Mose asked.

Jebediah replied, "To be followers of Christ, and we can't do that by holding on to things that don't matter when it comes to eternity."

Mose stood and walked to the end of the porch. "I'd like nothing more than our community to be united again. But I don't see that happening in my lifetime."

Jebediah moved to his side. "I've spent my whole life hoping I've been good enough to get to heaven. Over the past year, I've seen the light regarding our works-based salvation."

Jebediah laid his hand on his old friend's shoulder. "We're never going to be good enough if that is our only hope for heaven."

Mose jerked his shoulder away. "Do as you like. You'll go to hell with the rest of them."

Bishop Weaver turned his back, and Jebediah quietly left the porch and headed home.

Tracy Fredrychowski

CHAPTER 11

S imon counted every minute of every day during the week leading up to Sunday services. Taking time on Saturday to wash and clean his buggy, he hoped Anna would allow him the privilege of driving her home from the youth *singeon* on Sunday night. Anything to earn her trust back was a start. He wasn't sure if she still attended, but it was worth a shot.

Early Sunday morning Simon turned his horse and buggy over to the boys charged in caring for the rigs; Simon made his way to the side of the barn where the men had gathered. All dressed in black vests and starched Sunday best white shirts, the men spoke of weather and crops while waiting to file into the Yoders' home.

As the women walked past the barn and into the bank basement, Simon kept his eyes open for Anna. When he saw

Rebecca, but not Anna, he blew a silent breath through his lips. Maybe he had missed her. His current prayer was she would be in attendance.

His *bruder*, Benjamin, elbowed him and nodded his head toward their father's buggy. "True to his word, here come *Datt* and *Mamm*."

"Other than Bishop Schrock's new preaching style, I don't think they'll find the New Order Fellowship service much different from the Old Order."

Benjamin lowered his voice and leaned in closer to Simon. "Ya think any of the older boys will make the switch?"

"I couldn't say. Seems like each one of them needed to give it some serious thought. Many of their wives have families in the Old Order. It would mean more separation, for sure and certain."

Simon followed his *bruder's* eyes as they fell on Bella walking across the yard. Benjamin noted, "All I know is I'm glad we ain't married yet, so we can pick a wife from this church. That way, there's no questioning." There was no denying Benjamin's reasoning, and he hoped to do the same.

Stepping in line according to age had been a tradition Simon didn't mind following, as was sitting with the men on the opposite side of the room. There were several long-lived Amish traditions the New Order Fellowship adopted, and a few they didn't. But he had to agree it was nice seeing the women dressed in brighter colors than the drab, dark blue and burgundy.

However, nothing mattered more than following scripture and spreading the word of Jesus more openly. If their culture was going to survive, it would be changes like the one Bishop Schrock and the newly appointed ministers encouraged that would grow their followers. Just having a church full of the younger members of Willow Springs was encouragement enough in his books.

After Simon shook Daniel Miller's hand, the man to his immediate left, he found his place on the bench and scoured the women's side of the church. He closed his eyes as he picked up the *Ausbund* songbook from his seat to stifle his disappointment.

***

Anna pushed Steven's stroller along the winding sidewalk lined by the cliff overlooking Lake Erie. Bright sun rays broke through the trees and added to the serene landscape. It had been a week since arriving at the Buckhannons', and she could already tell Steven was responding to her care. Just that morning, she'd been able to get him to take a few bites of baby cereal before he finished a whole bottle. And to her surprise, not one ounce was wasted or spit up. An improvement for sure.

While she missed Mary Ellen and John Paul, Steven was also making a way in her heart. His curly dark hair and big brown eyes gave her purpose, something she hadn't felt since her *mamm* died. Perhaps God sent her to take care of him to show her she did have a reason in life, even if it might not be raising a family of her own.

Nearing the back entrance, feathery wisps of snow started falling, and Steven reached up and tried to grab the frozen crystals. His infectious baby-like giggle landed on her, full of joy and peace. At that moment, she wouldn't have wanted to be anywhere else.

She knelt near his stroller and held out her tongue until a dime-shaped snowflake landed and melted just as quickly. Mimicking her actions, he fumbled with his tongue as he reached out to her face. Catching his tiny fingers, she kissed them and said, "Your little mitts are cold. Best get you back inside. There will be plenty of snow for another day, I promise."

Setting the lock on the wheel, Anna picked Steven up and whispered calming words in his ear as she carried him inside. Mr. Buckhannon sat at the bar separating the kitchen from the breakfast nook, reading the paper. Looking over his glasses perched low on his nose, he said, "You're a natural. Not sure how we got so lucky finding you, but I'm glad we did."

Over the last week, the Buckhannons became more like friends than employers. Their friendly mannerisms and giving her free will to care for the child as she saw fit made for a comfortable work environment.

Anna shifted Steven to her hip and wiggled out of one side of her coat and then the other. When she hung it on the hook near the back door, she couldn't help but ask. "I'm sure there are nanny services here in Erie. Why did you look for a nanny so far away?"

Mr. Buckhannon folded his newspaper, laid it aside, and picked up his coffee. "We'd heard great things about Amish nannies, and we only wanted the best for Steven."

Anna shyly smiled. "But why me? I didn't have any formal training or references I could give you."

"I knew from the moment I met you. And besides, you were the answer to our prayers. We had just prayed for God to send us the perfect person to care for him, and twenty minutes later, you called. If that wasn't a sign from God, I don't know what else was."

Steven yawned and rubbed his tiny fingers across his nose. "Looks like all that fresh air did this little guy in. If you'll excuse me, I'll put him down for a nap, and then I'll be back to take care of the stroller."

"I'll put things away. You just tend to the baby."

Anna shook her head and smiled. As she walked through the kitchen and into the hallway, she thanked God for guiding her to the Buckhannons. They could have picked any other Amish community in the tri-state area but chose Willow Springs; for that, she would ever be grateful.

Mrs. Buckhannon called from her place on the sofa as she passed the living room. "Anna, I haven't seen Steven all morning. Please bring him to me."

Anna whispered in his ear. "Just a few more minutes, little one, and you can take that much-needed nap."

Mrs. Buckhannon held her arms out to Steven, and he leaned into Anna's shoulder. When Anna tried to pass him to Margaret again, the child held tighter and started to cry.

Defeated, Margaret dropped her hands and said, "I suppose that's my fault. I haven't been the most welcoming to him. Neal cared for Steven the most before you came along. He's not comfortable with me."

Anna didn't know what to say to the woman's confession. "I'm sorry. Maybe we should spend more time with you, and he'll get more comfortable. That might be all it takes. Children can sense pain and uneasiness. Steven might have picked up on that if you've been in a lot of agony."

Margaret's face dropped, and a glistening of moisture clouded her eyes. "Oh, I've been in pain, but most has been emotional."

The woman pulled the blanket up under her chin and turned away from Anna. "You can go now. Looks like he needs a nap anyways."

It seemed like the air in the room turned cold at Mrs. Buckhannon's comment. Something was bothering the woman, and if Anna could find a way to ease the woman's emotional pain when it came to Steven, she surely would try.

***

Margaret lay on the sofa, watching the flames bounce around the fire and thought back over the last six months. Such a short time for things in her life to change so dramatically. A quick shopping trip turned into a devastating car wreck, which took her only daughter's life and left her unable to care for her only grandchild. Finally, things had started to get better after almost a year of constant upheaval at her daughter's unplanned pregnancy. Why was God punishing her so? Wasn't it enough that he took her daughter, but he wasn't going to allow Steven to form a lasting bond with her? Why had life gotten so unbearable?

At this point, she was tired of fighting with both God and Neal. Whether Simon could prove he was a fit father or not, maybe Neal was right; Steven belonged with him. Especially since they couldn't keep someone like Anna caring for their grandson indefinitely. Besides, if Anna was any indication of how the Amish raised their children, what harm would come of allowing Steven to be brought up Amish.

All the time she had spent lying around, Margaret started questioning her motives for keeping Steven from his father. Wasn't it her own daughter who confessed to tricking Simon into sleeping with her in the first place? Cora knew Simon didn't handle alcohol well, but she spiked his drink anyways.

Simon wanted to do right by her daughter and the baby. But in the end, Cora refused to allow him to marry her after finding out he had planned to return to his Amish community and marry his childhood sweetheart. Cora wouldn't settle for second best for anything, especially Simon's heart.

The never-ending pain of losing Cora never entirely left her. She had learned to push all memories so deep there was no trace of Cora's face to pull from. After coming home from the hospital, she made Neal take every remembrance of their daughter and lock them away in her room at the end of the hall.

Maybe one day she could open the door and find comfort in the things that reminded her of her only daughter. But for now, she'd hide in pain with forced hellos and fake smiles.

***

Anna was awakened by Steven's early chatter during the break of the horizon that comes right before dawn. She rolled over and stayed as quiet as she could. Initially, she wanted to rush to his side. Still, he needed to learn to occupy himself and not demand her attention at every whim.

Amish children were taught early on that their existence was a gift from God, but that didn't mean the world revolved around them entirely. It took all her better judgment not to follow the pattern the Buckhannon's had already put in place by giving in to his every whim. But it took everything she had to follow through with their line of dealing with the crying child.

Anna made her way to his crib just as his gurgles turned into a full-fledged scream. When he laid his eyes on her, he sat up and reached out; her heart melted. Rebecca's words echoed in her ears. *"What happens if you become too attached to a child that's not yours? I would think that would be harder than you can imagine."*

Anna tried to reason with herself. *Perhaps I have a soft spot for the little one, but maybe that's because my heart is aching and empty for a child of my own. When the time is right, I'm sure I'll be able to leave him and go on with my life. I'm sure*

I'll be sad, who wouldn't be? But right now, he's filling me with joy. And besides, I believe the Lord wants me here.

***

After breakfast and a clean change of clothes, Anna carried Steven into the front room and sat him on the floor next to Margaret. "I thought perhaps we could spend some time in here with you for a spell…that is, if you are feeling up to it."

Mrs. Buckhannon gazed off into the fire. "I see no harm in you both enjoying the warmth."

Not the response Anna had hoped for, but she would take the little the woman offered. "He's starting to pull himself up. Look!" Anna let Steven wrap his hands around her fingers and remained firm as he pulled himself up.

A slight upturn of Margret's lip gave Anna hope, and the woman replied, "Well look at that. I'd say he's getting stronger."

"He just needed a little encouragement and some floor time."

"Floor time?"

Anna smiled. "Time to roll around and explore. Before we know it, we won't be able to stop him."

With a gulf of emotion, Margaret added, "We haven't had a little one in the house for a long time. I suppose we forgot a lot."

Steven plopped down, turned to his stomach, and pulled himself up on all fours, rocking back and forth. "See what I mean? It won't be long, and he'll crawl all over the place."

The look on the older woman's face confused Anna, and she asked, "You had other children?"

"Just one," returned Margret thoughtfully. "But we weren't around much when she was little. We had a nanny to take care of most things."

Mrs. Buckhannon grinned and then asked, "What is he doing?"

Anna smiled as Steven fell to his tummy and pulled himself back up on all fours. "He's learning to crawl."

As the two women enjoyed watching the little guy perform his new trick, Margret asked, "Do you plan on having children one day?"

"Lots, I hope."

"How many is that?"

Anna thought for a moment. "Oh…I don't know. I suppose however many God allows."

With a rise in her tone, Mrs. Buckhannon asked, "You don't determine that before marrying?"

Anna giggled, "No, we leave that up to God."

Margaret straightened her lap blanket and picked up a needlepoint project. "I guess that's one of the differences between the Amish and English."

After a thoughtful pause, Anna went on. "One of many, I suspect."

Margaret asked, "Do you mind if I ask a personal question?"

Anna helped Steven sit upright. "Of course not."

"You are so good with him; why aren't you married yet with your own babies?"

A twinge of regret constricted Anna's throat, and she had to swallow hard before answering. "I think God has other plans for my life right now. I'm trying to depend solely on the Lord's guidance and not rush into anything."

"That's quite commendable for such a young girl. I'm impressed."

"Oh, don't be. I have many faults when it comes to trusting in God. For years, I've wanted everything my way, on my timetable. When I didn't get it, I let myself be consumed with worry and anxiety." Anna let out a nervous sigh. "Most times, I have to remind myself I don't know better than Him."

Steven rolled over and picked up a toy to chew on. "Besides, I'm enjoying taking care of your son. He's been good for me. The more I concentrate on him, the less I worry about what's happening at home."

Margaret stopped weaving a needle through the canvas. "My son? Oh, I think you misunderstood; Steven is our grandson."

Anna pulled her knees up to her chest. "I'm sorry. I assumed you were his mother. May I ask where his parents are?"

Margaret spoke slowly. "His mother passed away in a car accident six months ago."

"And his father? Where is he?"

An edge in her voice gave Anna the impression Mrs. Buckhannon wasn't too fond of Steven's father.

"Hopefully, he's getting things in place to step up and take responsibility for his actions."

"I don't understand."

"Steven's biological father had some growing up to do, so we've given him six months to prove to us that he can be responsible."

"That makes sense now why you only need me for a few months."

"With any luck, the boy, while really he's a man, will come through and prove we can trust him to raise Steven right."

Anna crossed her legs and added, "I'm sorry about your daughter. I bet you miss her terribly."

A slight sob escaped Margaret's lips. "I do. We hadn't always seen eye-to-eye, but we were finally making a breakthrough after the baby was born. She had calmed down some and wasn't so wild. I think having Steven changed her."

Anna looked tenderly at Steven. "Does he favor your daughter?"

Mrs. Buckhannon studied the child's face. "He looks a lot like his father. His curly dark hair and face shape, but those brown eyes are all his mother's." Anna smiled as the woman lovingly pondered over her grandson.

"So, how did you end up with Steven and not his father in the first place?"

"It's a long story and one I'm not proud to tell, but in a nutshell, they weren't married."

"Oh, my. I'm sorry."

"Those things happen, especially with my daughter. She was known to do whatever it took to get her way. I suppose that is half my fault. Her father and I didn't do too good of a job raising her. She spent more time in boarding schools than with us. But in the end, she tricked the boy's father. He didn't even know about him until after he was born."

"I hope it works out."

"So do we. The young man comes from a good family, and we think it's just a matter of time before he gets everything in place to care for him. But, enough about that. I want to learn more about you. Tell me a little about yourself."

"Not much to tell. What do you want to know?"

"Let's start with, is there anyone special in Willow Springs waiting for you?"

Anna looked away, busied herself with Steven, and muttered, "Maybe."

"Tell me about Mr. Maybe."

She snickered and said, "It's a long story, and one I'm not proud to tell." Both women laughed.

"Mr. Maybe left for a few years and has just returned home, and he wants to pick up where we left off."

"And you don't want that?"

"It's not that. He...he left me a few days before we were to be married. I'm not so sure I can trust him again."

"What are you afraid of? If he came back to claim you and your heart is still open, why wouldn't you want to at least explore it?"

"He broke my heart, and it took me years to get over him."

Anna let out a small sigh. "He swears he never stopped loving me and always planned to return."

Mrs. Buckhannon raised her eyebrows. "I'd say if it's been a few years and you didn't let anyone else step in and take your heart, you haven't gotten over him."

"Perhaps. That's why I decided to take this job. I hoped that if I got away for a while, I could hear God's voice clearer, and he would guide me to which path he wanted me to take."

"So, what is Mr. Maybe's name?"

"Simon, Simon Kauffman."

Margaret dropped her needlepoint on her lap and let out a small gasp. Anna turned at the sound. "Everything all right?"

"Ohh…oh yes, my dear. Looks like Steven's ready for his morning nap, and I'd also like to rest for a while."

Anna stood and picked up Steven and his toys. "This was nice. Would you like us to visit with you later this afternoon again?"

Margaret nodded and added, "That would be nice. Can you go to Neal's study and let him know I'd like to have a word with him when he gets a break from his work?"

"Yes, ma'am. Anything else you need before I go?"

"No, I don't think so. But Anna."

"Yes?"

"I think God sent you exactly where you need to be."

Mrs. Buckhannon reached out and squeezed Anna's hand lovingly. "You are the answer to our prayers."

Anna headed to the study at the back of the house, balancing Steven over her hip as she went. It was good to see Mrs. Buckhannon at ease with her, especially after her blue mood the day before. Perhaps God did have a purpose in sending her to the Buckhannon's.

CHAPTER 12

O utside, the snow glistened in the morning sunshine. In the distance, Simon waited as Benjamin tried maneuvering the manure spreader out of the barn. It was two weeks before Christmas, and Simon was beside himself. Only three more weeks before his hearing date, and he wasn't even close to proving anything to the Buckhannons.

Benjamin hollered his direction. "I could use some help over here!"

Simon followed his *bruder's* voice and reached out to settle the two Belgian horses struggling to back the full spreader out of the narrow double doors. "Isn't it too early to spread this? I'm not sure the ground is even frozen enough yet."

Benjamin bellowed, "We've managed fine without you for the last three years; now is not the time to tell us how we need to do things."

"Whoa, there! I'm doing no such thing; I just don't want you to get this thing buried in mud."

"And you don't think these guys are strong enough to pull it out if we do?"

Jebediah came around the corner, shovel in hand. "What's all the yelling about?"

Benjamin picked up the reins and guided the horses around Simon. "Mr. Hotshot here thinks he knows it all. Maybe you can convince him otherwise."

Simon jumped back and moved to his father's side. "Sorry about that. I think I might have stepped on his toes."

Jebediah headed back into the barn with Simon on his heels. "I think the boy has girl trouble. He's been in a foul mood all morning."

Simon let the first cow in the row out of its stanchion and led him to the door. Morning milking was complete, and the cows were free to move outside, giving Simon and his older *bruder's* ample room to clean the stalls.

A chill in the air mixed with steam coming off fresh manure allowed Simon time to clear his head. He needed to figure out a way to spend time with Anna. On more than one occasion over the last few weeks, he wanted to ask Eli if he had any word about when Anna planned to come home. Not knowing if Anna had shared things with Rebecca kept him from probing too deep.

As he made his way down the cement-lined barn, he worked at scraping manure into the cow alley. Only stopping when he reached the end of the twenty-stanchion row, he removed his hat and wiped his brow with the back of his hand.

His father came out of the cement block milk house and sat on a hay bale. "Keep that up, and you won't have any need for your *bruders* and me."

Simon pushed his bangs off his forehead and replaced his straw hat. "Some days, I need hard work to sort things out."

Jebediah snorted and pointed to the bucket beside him. "Take a seat, son. There's plenty of work for all of us. No one said you have to do it alone."

Simon looked around the barn and noticed his five older *bruders* working in unison, laughing, and cutting up on each other, oblivious to his sudden burst of energy.

"What's got you all worked up today?"

Kicking a glob of wet straw off his boots, Simon took off his gloves and rested them on his knee. "I'm running out of time."

His father nodded at one of his eldest son's jokes and asked, "I didn't know you were privy to God's timetable."

"*Nee.*"

His *datt* smiled cryptically and stood. "I didn't think so."

His father's wise words were all it took to get Simon's head back in line with God's plan.

***

Anna brushed snow off Steven's snowsuit before setting him down on the rug just inside the back door. "I'm not sure who had more fun just now, you or me." Steven whimpered and held his hands up. "I know, little one; let me get out of my coat first."

Mr. Buckhannon came to her rescue; he picked his grandson up and wiggled him free from the cumbersome layer of warmth. "Did you have fun sitting in the snow with Anna?"

The child rubbed his nose with his tiny fist and leaned back toward Anna. After hanging her coat up and slipping out of her boots, she pulled Steven back into her arms. "I do believe I wore the little guy out."

Mr. Buckhannon asked, "Do you think it's a good idea to have him out in the cold for so long?"

Anna walked to the sink to make a bottle and tipped her head in his direction. "Children need sunshine, and a little cold air never hurt anyone."

Neal shrugged his shoulders and smiled. "I suppose you're right, but our daughter's nanny hated the cold, so she never took her outside to play."

"In my community, we encourage our children to be outside as much as possible. Even at this age."

"I'll take your word for it. I can tell he's thriving under your care, so I trust you."

Steven took the bottle and threw his head back on Anna's shoulder. "I'd say all that fresh air has more than one benefit."

"He'll be out in less than ten minutes," Anna expressed.

Mr. Buckhannon picked up a stack of mail. "After settling him, will you meet with Margaret and me in the living room? We have something we'd like to discuss with you."

Anna moved Steven in her arms to a more comfortable position and replied, "Of course."

***

Once Steven had fallen asleep, Anna went to the front room where Mrs. Buckhannon was waiting.

"That was quick," Mrs. Buckhannon smiled and pointed to the chair near the sofa.

"Steven had a big breakfast and enjoyed the time outside. I knew it wouldn't be long, and he'd be fast asleep." Anna said.

Margaret only smiled, then Neal, who had just stepped in, added, "You've been so good for the boy, and we don't know what we would have done had you not answered our ad. We just want you to know how pleased we are with the progress you've made with him over the last month."

Unaccustomed to praise, Anna shyly added, "You have no idea how much fun I've had caring for him. He is such a sweet boy and has brought me such joy."

Margaret added, "We've noticed you thoroughly enjoy him. So different from our daughter's nanny. That woman acted as if she was a bother. Whereas you've put your whole soul into his care. We want you to know how much we appreciate loving him like you do."

"Really, he's an easy child to love."

Mr. Buckhannon took a seat in the wingback chair that mirrored Anna's. "We asked you to meet with us because we have a little problem we hope you can help us solve."

Anna didn't answer but listened intently.

"Margaret's doctor wants her to consult with a spine specialist in Atlanta in two days. He hopes this new doctor agrees with his prognosis. If he does, she'll need another surgery in Atlanta."

"Oh, no. How can I help?"

Mrs. Buckhannon added a bookmark to the book she was reading and laid it aside. "We aren't comfortable leaving you alone in this big house so far from home. We hope you'll agree to take Steven back to your sister's until after the first of the year."

"You want me to take him to Willow Springs?"

Neal asked, "Do you think your family would mind?"

Anna thought for a moment and smiled. "I think that would be a wonderful idea. My niece, Mary Ellen, would love another playmate. And I'd like nothing more than to introduce Steven to my family. I'm sure they would love it."

Margaret winked in Neal's direction. "We hate that we'll be gone over Christmas, but I'm sure Steven won't even realize we're gone. He's grown quite attached to you."

Anna flushed. "I hope that doesn't bother you."

"Heaven's no. If it weren't for you, we'd still be doing everything wrong because we thought we knew best. But now we see he is much happier with you in his life."

"Good, I certainly don't want to take your place."

Neal nodded in agreement. "No one can take our place. But someone can certainly do a better job of raising him than us. We are much too old to take on that responsibility full-time. And until his father gets his life together, we're counting on you to see to Master Steven's wellbeing."

Anna crossed her leg, weaved her fingers around her knee, and asked, "When are you leaving?"

The older woman responded, "We leave tomorrow afternoon. And if you agree to take Steven home with you, Neal will call our driver and hire him to take you home this evening."

"Today? I'll need to get things packed and ready to go." Anna stood. "I'm honored you both trust me with your grandson, and I promise to take good care of him while you're away."

Neal smiled and responded, "We know you will, and we wouldn't trust Steven's care to anyone else."

As Anna left the room and up the stairs, Neal turned to Margaret and asked, "Are you sure we shouldn't tell her we know about her connection with Simon? Won't it be awkward when she shows up with his baby?"

"Oh, Neal, you worry too much. Simon's not going to recognize him. The child was only a few weeks old when he saw him last. Steven has a full head of hair now, and I doubt the child even had his eyes open when Simon held him. And other than the picture Cora sent him of the two of them, he'll not recognize Steven Marcus."

Margaret paused for a few seconds while she shifted on the sofa. "I'm certain he won't put two and two together and figure it out. Besides, Cora introduced Steven as Marcus, so I'm certain the boy calls him Marcus, not Steven."

Mr. Buckhannon shook his head. "I feel like we're deceiving the girl, and I'm not sure I like it."

Margaret patted the back of her husband's hand. "When it comes to heart matters, you let me figure that out. And after all we went through with losing Cora, I feel we need to give Steven the best chance at life as we can."

Neal covered his wife's hand and squeezed gently. "You really think Steven's best shot in life is being raised Amish? They live such a backward way of life."

"Backward to who? You and me? I've never met a girl quite like Anna. She's pretty special, and if Simon holds even an ounce of similar values as Anna, how can that be wrong?"

Neal sighed, and Margaret beseeched him. "Look, Neal, I know it will be hard to let him go, but I promised myself months ago that if I had the chance to make things up to Cora for all the wrong I did while she was growing up, I would. I believe God sent Anna here so I could make things right."

"But what about college and a good education? They don't encourage their children to get an education past eighth grade?"

Margaret whispered tenderly, "Let's cross that bridge when we get to it." Gradually, Margaret continued, "What good did all that schooling do for Cora? All it did was expose her to all kinds of things that we wish she wouldn't have explored.

Perhaps we're the ones who have it all wrong. Maybe separating our children from the world isn't bad after all. It certainly hasn't hurt Anna. By talking with her about her family and church, I see a loving community where children prosper. How can that be wrong?"

Neal covered her hand with his other. "I trust your judgment on this one. But I don't understand how keeping all we know from Anna is right."

Margaret assured him. "God is already at work here, and He doesn't need our help. If His plan is for the two of them to work things out, then I trust He'll make it happen. We're just putting the pieces in place; it's His job to line them up perfectly."

***

Two hours later, Anna stood in the hallway while Mr. Buckhannon gave Steven a kiss on his forehead and wished them both well. The driver had already carried their bags to the car and was securing Steven's car seat in the backseat.

"Do you have everything?" Mr. Buckhannon gave her an envelope with money in it. "I want you to take this, and if he needs anything, use this. I wrote my cell phone number on the outside. If you need whatsoever, you call me, and I'll send whatever you need."

"Really you don't need to do that. I'll have everything I require at Rebecca and Eli's."

"I'll not take no for an answer. I don't want you to put your family out in the least."

She laughed. "Put them out? I hardly doubt that. They will be overjoyed we've come to stay, especially with Christmas so close. I wish I had time to let them know we were coming."

In a concerned tone, Neal asked, "Do you think it will be a problem?"

"A problem? No. I just know Rebecca, and she will have wanted to have everything just perfect upon our arrival."

After fastening Steven in his seat and slipping in beside him, Anna leaned around his chair and waved at Mr. Buckhannon. He stood on the front porch until they pulled away.

Anna gave Margaret ample time to visit with Steven before she left and caught the woman wiping away a few tears. The older woman's outlook changed entirely after the day they spent getting to know one another. Anna understood more about Mrs. Buckhannon's guilt and tried to help her work through her pain.

Anna looked back toward the old Victorian one last time before the driver pulled onto the highway. For some odd reason, it was like she was seeing the house for the last time. A twinge of sadness settled quickly but left as fast as it came when Steven reached out and touched her cheek.

She leaned in and kissed his tiny fingers. "You'll have the best time getting to know John Paul and Mary Ellen. And Rebecca and Eli are going to love you as their own. Mary Ellen will try to mother you just like she does John Paul."

Anna leaned back in her seat and took in a deep, cleansing breath. It was good to be going home, but it brought an onslaught of worry about facing Simon. She'd been so busy with Steven that she hardly thought about what was facing her back in Willow Springs. Except for the few times Simon's face and the mysterious dark-haired child made their way back into her dreams.

As she turned back to study Steven, a small gasp made its way to the hollow of Anna's throat. The boy who filled the hours right before she awoke looked much like the child filling her days between dawn and dusk.

***

Just before eight, the driver pulled into Eli and Rebecca's driveway. The warm glow from the single gas lamp in her *schwester's* front window made Anna giddy. She unhooked Steven's seat and stepped out of the car. A swirl of chimney smoke encased her nose, and she followed the light to the front door.

Before she could open it, Eli stepped out onto the porch. "Anna? We wondered who would be calling this late at night."

"I know; I didn't have time to leave a message. But I've come home to spend the holidays with everyone."

"That's *gut* news. Rebecca will be pleased. She's putting the *kinner* to bed. Go in, and I'll help the driver with your bags."

Rebecca's home was welcoming, and the matching rockers were moved closer to the wood stove in the living room. The cookstove's oven door had been left open in the kitchen, and Eli's gloves and hat were hanging on a drying rack above the stove.

Steven hadn't stirred, and she laid him on the daybed in the kitchen corner while she removed her winter clothing. She had missed the coziness of her *schwester's* home and thanked God for allowing her to return safely. Untying Steven's hat and unzipping his snowsuit, she moved him to the side of the daybed. Rebecca loved to have the children close and often used the daybed for quick naps or cuddle time.

Anna rushed to the door to help Eli just as Rebecca came down the stairs. "Anna, you're home. Why didn't you tell me? I would have gotten your room ready for you."

"It happened so quickly I barely had time to pack, let alone get a message to you." Anna grabbed her *schwester's* hand. "Come see what I've brought with me."

Anna put her finger to her lip and whispered, "Shhh...he's sleeping, but Mr. and Mrs. Buckhannon let me bring Steven."

Rebecca smiled and leaned over the sleeping child. "Look at those curls. He is the cutest thing ever. Oh...Mary Ellen is going to be so excited."

"*Jah*, I know."

"How long are you staying?"

Anna pulled Rebecca back into the front room. "Mrs. Buckhannon had to go to Atlanta for her back, so I'm here until she is back home. Most likely a few weeks." Anna paused. "I hope that's all right?"

"Of course, it is. Don't you agree, Eli?"

Eli opened the door to the brown metallic wood box in the living room and raked the coals together before adding a few pieces of wood to the pile. "We're so glad to have you home,

Anna, and I can't think of anything better than to have another child in the house."

"I told you." Rebecca linked her arm to Anna's. "Come, let's make some tea, and you can tell me all about the little guy."

CHAPTER 13

M ilking time at the Kauffman farm picked back up as soon as supper was over. Simon and Benjamin followed their *datt* to the barn, where Jebediah pushed the button to the milk house and started the diesel engine. Simon began sanitizing the milkers and Benjamin started to herd the one hundred Holstein into their stanchions. The older boys showed up and found their places throughout the barn.

It didn't take Simon long to become a welcomed addition back on his father's dairy farm, and he worked hard to prove himself to his *bruders* and his *datt*.

Benjamin hollered over the head of a cow in Simon's direction. "I've been meaning to ask if old man Mast needs any help at the lumber mill."

Simon stopped momentarily from washing out the inside of the milk tank to respond. "Who wants to know?"

"I do!"

Simon chuckled. "It's hard work. You think you're up for that?"

Benjamin hollered over the herd of Holsteins, finding their way to their stanchions, one after another. "I suspect if you can handle it, anyone can. Besides, it's good money, and I need to make some extra cash."

Simon hollered back, "I'm ready to give my notice, so I bet you can take my place."

"What? You're quitting?"

Simon lifted his head in his father's direction. "It's time I start building on that piece of land *Datt* gave me, and I don't have time to do all three. Work here, at the mill, and build a house. There's only so much time in a day."

"Why do you need extra cash all of a sudden?" Simon asked.

"The same reason you want to leave. It's time I step up and make something of myself. And that takes money. It's one thing *Datt* giving us land, but it's another if we want to build on it."

Each cow knew exactly where she belonged. Simon's oldest *bruder* chained the cow's metal stanchion around each neck and remarked, "It's about time!"

Jebediah shoveled grain into a long trough that lined the barn. "It's time you both contribute to the next generation of Kauffman boys*, jah?*"

Simon lowered his eyes, and his mind went to Anna. He picked up the sprayer to drown out their voices as he hosed out the milk tank.

After seeing that his sons had everything under control, Jebediah followed Simon into the cement block milk house, closed the door, and sat on an overturned bucket. "*Mamm* saw Rebecca Bricker at the Mercantile this afternoon."

"*Jah?*"

"Anna's back."

Simon snapped his head up. "For good?"

"Don't think so. Seems she's brought a child back with her."

"Ohhh…"

"That's not the worst of it."

"How so?"

"Rebecca mentioned the child's name to your *mamm*."

"*Jah*, so what does that mean to me?"

"She referred to him as eight-month-old Master Steven Buckhannon."

Simon dropped the hose and ran toward the house to speak to his mother.

***

Naomi knew long before she heard the heavy steps on the porch who was about to enter her kitchen. Her after-supper discussion with Jebediah was sure to cause an uproar in the barn, for sure and certain. She dried her hands on a towel and turned toward the door.

"*Datt* just told me you saw Rebecca this afternoon. Tell me it ain't true. Tell me Anna hasn't been caring for Marcus all this time."

"Calm down, Simon. Ain't no use getting yourself all worked up over nothing."

"Nothing? How can you say it's nothing? This just lays another layer of stuff I must dig through to earn her trust. I hadn't told her about Marcus yet."

"I told you she needed to know. I still don't understand your reasoning behind keeping something so important from her."

"I didn't want him to be the reason. I wanted it to be us alone."

Naomi slid down in a chair at the table and wrung the dishtowel in her hands. "I just don't know, son. I think you should have been honest with her from the start."

"Ohhh...*Mamm*, this just complicates things even more."

"*Nee*, what muddied things is you not being forthright with her from the start."

He raised his voice slightly. "How can I do that if the woman won't give me the time of day?"

Naomi crossed her arms.

Simon took a seat next to his mother and lowered his head. "I'm sorry, *Mamm*. I'm so frustrated with the whole situation. I'm trying hard to let God handle things, but all I see are roadblocks."

His mother smiled, and he asked, "What?"

"You see roadblocks; I see the Lord paving a way into Anna's heart."

"How so?"

"Come on, Simon, open your eyes. How did your son end up with Anna despite all the jobs and the young girls who take nanny jobs in this community?"

He leaned back in his chair and bounced his fingers on the table. "*Jah*, I think you're right."

"There's no thinking about it. God has his hands all over this. And if you can't see that, you're just plain crazy."

Simon relaxed a little in his chair and asked, "Now what?"

Naomi stood and walked back to the sink. "Seems like the good Lord didn't need your help thus far; he surely doesn't need it now."

Simon pushed in his chair and headed toward the door. "Best get back out there."

"Son."

"*Jah*?"

"You already gave it over to Him once, don't go picking it back up. He doesn't need your help. Keep praying, be in His Word, and trust His will, His way."

Simon tipped his head and smiled as he went out the door. The temperature continued to drop, and air burned his chest as he returned to the barn. He couldn't help but yearn to hitch up the buggy and pay a visit to the Bricker house. But he would heed his mother's advice and let God show him what to do next.

While the cows were being milked, Simon went to the hayloft and threw bales through the hole in the barn floor. He also threw the corn fodder down they would use for bedding once milking was complete.

When Benjamin removed the milker from the last cow, he helped Simon clear the gutters in the floor of manure. At the same time, the older boys continue to ready the milk for the five o'clock milk tanker arrival.

Now that the cows were ready for the night, the boys could relax and prepare for the whole thing to start over in twelve short hours. Dairy farming was hard, but Simon enjoyed the grueling work. He couldn't think of anything else than how it would provide a steady income for his future family. He prayed that God would soften Anna's heart and she would fall in love with Marcus and agree to make a life with both of them.

While that was his ultimate dream, he could only imagine how she would handle the truth once it was revealed. An empty hole in the pit of his stomach turned as he thought about how easy it had been to keep the truth from her. Was he ever going to learn that honesty was always the best choice?

He heaved a long sigh as he climbed the stairs to his bedroom. Even the hot shower did little to wash the concern from his mind. Anna didn't like to be deceived, and he was afraid he may have made it worse by keeping Marcus a secret from her.

His damp hair stuck to his forehead, and he brushed it aside as he picked up the picture on his nightstand. The only time he met his son was when Cora told him of his existence. She died shortly after, leaving him to independently sort out their son's future. That was almost seven months ago, and he couldn't formulate a clear picture of what he might look like now.

He certainly wouldn't need to wait long since he was sure they both would attend church in the morning. It was like moving boulders to get the Buckhannon's to consider him taking full custody. They didn't like him from the get-go, and he didn't blame them much since he left their daughter to bear the burden of their one-night stand by herself.

He rubbed his thumb over Steven Marcus's tiny figure in the picture and thought, *I promise son, I'll make this up to you and your momma. Anna will make a good mother, I'm sure of it. We just need to be patient and let God do His thing.*

***

Rebecca giggled at the mess Steven had made on his tray. "I think he'd do just as well by himself."

Anna sighed and let him twist the spoon out of her hand. When it hit the floor, he laughed aloud. Both women joined him in his amusement.

"Such a trickster for a nine-month-old," Rebecca commented as she shifted John Paul over her shoulder. "I can tell he will light his own way."

"Most days, I let him get used to a spoon, but I'm anxious this morning."

"Why's that?"

"I think the whole idea of taking him to church has me all flustered. What if I can't keep him quiet and he starts to fuss?"

"Now, Anna, you're getting all worked up about nothing. You've quieted more than one fussy baby in your lifetime, and Steven won't be any different."

"But he's never had to stay quiet for so long. You see how busy he is; he's not happy unless he's exploring."

"Then let him explore. Bishop Schrock and the rest of the ministers are much more laid back than Bishop Weaver. I don't think you have anything to worry about."

Anna wiped the child's face with a towel and looked at the clock. "Oh heavens, I'm not even dressed yet. Eli will have the buggy pulled around any minute."

Rebecca laid John Paul in the center of the daybed and shooed her *schwester* away. "I'll get Steven cleaned up. You go get dressed."

***

Snow fell in great feathery wisps as Anna handed Steven up to Rebecca. After she stepped into the backseat of Eli's family buggy, she pulled Mary Ellen close and balanced Steven on her knee. Eli walked around the horse, making sure the harness was secured. Rebecca turned in her seat and asked, "Do you think your edginess has anything to do with church being at the Kauffman's today?"

"I can't help feeling a little overwhelmed by it all."

Rebecca turned her attention to her husband, who was fastening down the side of the canvas curtain to keep out the December air, leaving Anna to sort out her apprehension alone.

The grinding of the steel wheels and the clopping of the horses' hooves got louder as Eli left the gravel driveway and pulled out onto the blacktopped road. A light layer of snow covered the road and added to the peacefulness of the line of buggies, all with a bright orange triangle on the back, making their way to the Kauffman's.

***

Jebediah stood back and watched all seven of his sons do their part in ensuring there wasn't one thing out of place on the Kauffman farm. This was the first time he had hosted church since switching his membership to the New Order Fellowship.

As he stood on the porch before dawn, Naomi met him with a cup of coffee. Taking the cup in one hand and pulling her in close, he asked, "Did you ever dream in all our years that each of our boys would follow us to this new church?"

Naomi looked up lovingly. "I'm not surprised. You've done a fine job of instilling the love of God in each one of our sons.

And besides, I've been praying for each of their families for the last couple of years."

"For two years?"

"*Jah*, I knew the day Henry, Eli, Samuel, and Daniel walked out of the Old Order that we'd follow someday."

"How could have you been so sure?"

"I'm not sure; I just knew. I haven't been married to you for this long, not knowing you live by the truth. That and Eli's grandmother, Mary, shared the truth of salvation with me long before that."

"She did, did she?"

"*Jah*, I knew it was just a matter of time until you got curious enough about what the young men were preaching that you found out for yourself."

He squeezed her tighter. "You're a good woman, Naomi Kauffman."

The soft glow of the battery-powered lights leading the way of a parade of buggies up Jebediah's driveway forced him to take a long sip of his coffee before handing the cup back to his wife.

"I'd say that's my call to the barn. You've got everything under control in the house?"

Naomi grinned. "Now Jebediah, you know me better than that. Moreover, before they went home, our daughters-in-law had everything laid out last night. I suspect they're in there now double-checking things."

***

Simon pulled his black waistcoat tighter and stepped out to meet the first family who had arrived. Bishop Schrock stopped at his side, and Simon reached to steady the horse while bidding each other good morning. Henry walked around, held his arms out to lift down his two children, and then held a hand to his wife, Maggie.

"*Gut* day for the Lord, *jah?*" Henry asked as Simon led the buggy away.

Simon nodded in his direction and countered, "This snow keeps up like this, and we may have to dig our way home in a few hours."

For the next thirty minutes, family after family pulled up to the Kaufmann farm. When Simon noticed Eli's carriage stop at the barn, he was the first to lend a hand in hopes of seeing Anna.

Stepping up to the carriage, Simon watched as Rebecca handed down her black train case diaper bag and John Paul to Eli before reaching back for Mary Ellen.

Waiting for Eli and Rebecca to step aside, Simon held his hand out to help Anna out of the back of the buggy. Struggling to balance Steven and pick up her train case simultaneously, Simon reached up and took Steven from her arms.

His son, smaller than he imagined, smelled of Anna. A hint of lavender and vanilla filled his nose as he balanced the child on his hip. To his surprise, the boy laid his head on his shoulder. The simple act warmed Simon's heart until Anna purposely avoided eye contact.

He pulled the child close before Anna took him from his arms. "*Denki*," she mouthed as she fell into step with Rebecca and Mary Ellen.

Simon followed Anna with his eyes as he led Eli's buggy away, watching as she lined up to enter the house, oldest to youngest, as they had done for centuries.

His stomach churned at the thought of Anna's reaction when she discovered what he'd kept from her. He prayed continually and found his place in line as the men entered the house.

The living room and kitchen of his parent's home were filled with people, all sitting expectantly on wooden benches. After allowing the men in front of him to find their seats, he sat at the end of the row, which happened to be directly across from Anna, who sat straight to his left. He struggled to keep his head forward with only a few feet between them.

After the first hymn ended, there was a pause before the song leader sang the first few words to the *Lob Lied,* the second song sung in every Amish service across the country. As the drawn-out hymn echoed on the bare walls, the ministers prepared for the morning service in an upstairs bedroom.

Few things had changed from the Old Order Service to the New Order Fellowship, except for following the scripture more closely and laying aside some of the rules of the *Ordnung.*

Simon enjoyed Bishop Schrock and the ministers preaching more from the Bible and sharing more about Jesus. Even the prepared message was understood better since it was taught in *Englisch* and not Old German. After the second song ended, he heard the minister's footsteps making their way back downstairs.

Out of the corner of his eye, he noticed Anna bouncing Marcus on her knee as he chewed on a small toy. She had removed his hat, revealing a layer of delicate dark curls. Simon moved his hand to the back of his head and matted the unruly waves, hoping Anna wouldn't notice the resemblance.

As Minister Yoder spoke, Simon struggled to concentrate on the message. However, Samuel stopped and emphasized his point. "Anyone who is born again will live for Christ, but those who are just living the life of a Christian are only living for themselves."

Simon forced his thoughts from the woman on his left and turned an ear to Samuel's final words. "If anyone here finds they are trusting their salvation on their outward Christian appearance, I encourage you to meet with me after service about being re-baptized in Jesus. Baptism should be a change of heart, not a ritual into adulthood."

As Minister Bricker took his place in front of the congregation, Simon noticed Anna struggling to keep Steven Marcus still. In hushed whispers, she relented, allowing the child to sit on the floor. Within seconds, he crawled across the break in the benches and pulled himself up to Simon's knee.

A quick look in Anna's direction met apologetic eyes, and without hesitation, he picked the child up. Letting his son stand on his lap to look over his shoulder, Simon tried to focus on what Eli was saying. "If we wash only on the outside but never address the inside, we as Christians will never amount to anything but a worldly, sinful people."

Simon thought, *Is that what I've done? Have I cleaned myself up well enough to look like an Amish Christian on the outside but ignored what's going on inside?*

Glancing only momentarily to Anna and then up to his father, who was intently listening to the service, he couldn't help but think about his *datt*. Not once had his father not put his family first, right after God, in everything he did.

Simon hoped that at one point, his son would gaze at him the same way. His father was a man who was clean both on the inside and out. He wanted to be that kind of person. He wanted to raise his son with the same moral values he'd learned as a child.

As Steven Marcus rubbed his nose and chin on Simon's shoulder, the child relaxed in his arms and laid his head in the crook of Simon's neck.

Never in his whole life had he felt so much responsibility for a child he barely knew, but something inside of him snapped to the point that he held the child tighter. Simon closed his eyes as he let Eli's words settle deep in his soul.

"Brothers and sisters, I plead with you to examine yourself. Being a Christian isn't about how we look on the outside. It's not our dress or coverings; it's not neat yards, straight rows, or even a set of rules that don't get us closer to heaven.

It's about how we share God's Word. It's about being honest about the condition of our hearts. Please remember what Jesus's instruction tells us. Love the Lord thy God and love your neighbor as yourself."

As soon as the last prayer was over, Anna stood and took the sleeping child from Simon's arms without uttering a word. Simon didn't move until Benjamin kicked the side of his boot, urging him along.

Anna disappeared into an upstairs bedroom. Simon helped a group of men turn the benches over to convert them to adjoining tables for lunch. Someone had lifted the cover off the large pot of simmering bean soup, filling the air with the pleasant aroma. Lingering as long as he could without getting in the way, Simon headed upstairs to grab a pair of gloves.

***

It was all Anna could do to escape Simon's longing eyes. His fresh scent remained embedded in Steven's hair long after she'd changed his diaper and fed him a bottle. Without realizing it, she had slipped into Simon's bedroom. The picture that had once hung from his rearview mirror was propped up against the gas light on his nightstand.

As she rocked Steven, she studied the picture. The young, dark-haired girl looked oddly familiar, and an edge of bitterness crept up her neck. The letter she had received from Cora over a year ago still played in her mind. For years, she had held onto the hope Simon would return to her, but in an instant and within a few lines on a piece of paper, all of her hopes and dreams washed away. And now, to find out Cora's letter was nothing more than a lie did little to ease her discomfort.

Her brother-in-law's words rang in her head. Perhaps Eli's words were meant for her, she thought. *Have I hidden behind my outward appearances without giving any thought to the actual condition of my heart? Have I been so angry with Simon I've entirely ignored God's teachings? I've forgiven him. Haven't I?*

At that moment, she felt no better than Cora by allowing her bitterness to put a wedge between her and Simon. She buried her nose in Steven's curls and took a deep breath, hoping to absorb more of Simon.

Closing her eyes, she prayed, *"Lord, only you know your plans for my life. Please fill my heart with joy and help me remember that your will is better than anything my human mind can conceive. Show me any area in my life where I'm not honoring you."*

When she opened her eyes, Simon stood in the doorway of his room. After stepping inside, he said in no more than a whisper, "I need to talk to you."

Anna put her finger to her lips to quiet him and gently laid Steven in the center of the bed. After patting his bottom to be sure he was asleep, she moved to the window, and Simon followed.

Shifting from one foot to another, Simon asked, "How have you been?"

Ignoring his question, she commented, *"Denki,* for helping me with Steven."

"It was nothing."

"It was something, especially since he's never gone so easily to someone else for as long as I've cared for him."

Simon glanced at the bed. "He's taken to you."

"*Jah*, I'm pretty fond of him myself."

Simon turned toward the window and then back toward the door when noise from downstairs seeped upward. "There is so much I need to explain to you, but this isn't the place."

Anna paused to steady her voice, then continued slowly. "Not too certain we have much to say to one another right now. I'm still trying to sort through all we've been through and the path the Lord might have me on."

Simon looked distressed. "And I'm trying to do the same. However, I haven't been quite honest with you about something."

All was quiet as Anna pushed down a wave of anxiety. She trembled to think what it might be and wasn't too sure she could handle another blow against her already raging heart.

Simon sighed when she dropped her head, rubbed her eyes, and said, "I'm not ready to hear what you might need to say, Simon. You must remember I waited for three years for you to come back and explain something…anything. But not a word, and now you're all antsy to confess something that you need to get off your chest."

Simon reached out to her, and she recoiled. "It's taken me this long to get over you, and you must realize it might take me just as long to decide if you are right for me again."

Simon dropped his arms to his side and watched as she picked up his son and left. The muscle in his jaw twitched as he let her slip away, unable to say a word to fix what his selfishness had caused.

CHAPTER 14

The following day, Simon received a letter from Mr. Buckhannon and two official papers. Confused, he glared at Mr. and Mrs. Buckhannon's signatures on both documents. Shuffling through the papers, he opened the handwritten note included.

Dear Simon,

With much sadness, I'm writing to inform you that Margaret and I can no longer care for Steven Marcus. After an intense medical examination, it has been determined that Margaret suffers from inoperable tumors on her spine. Her condition will continue to decline rapidly until she can no longer care for herself, much less Steven.

We are too old to continue giving Steven the care and attention he deserves. In place of our upcoming court date, we have instructed our lawyer to draw up the attached documents providing you with two options for Steven's continued care.

As you may have already figured out, we hired Anna Byler to care for Steven. We have come to love the young girl and know he will be safe with her until you decide what is best for your son's future.

Simon, I know we have not always made things easy for you, and we apologize for demanding you prove to us your worthiness. After spending so much time with Anna, we feel raising Steven as Amish would be in his best interest. And we also know Anna was the young lady you intended to marry before our Cora deceived you.

We pray you'll be able to work things out with Anna and trust you will do your best whatever you decide.

Please take time to seriously consider the enclosed two documents and determine what would be best for all concerned.

Sincerely,

Neal and Margaret Buckhannon

Simon carried the papers to his room and sat on the edge of his bed. The official documents bore a hole in his heart. He had been given two options. Accept full custody or put his son up for adoption.

He thought of nothing else but bringing Marcus home for months. But now, after Anna's continued refusal to hear him out, he didn't have much hope of reconciling Anna's heart. In his mind, taking on the responsibility of raising the boy hinged on her being his wife. Would it be in his son's best interests to accept custody if he meant he had to do it alone?

Maybe the Buckhannons gave him the option to sign over his parental right because that would be the child's best chance for everyday life. At least then, the child could be adopted into a loving family where both mother and father could be present.

Simon dropped the papers to the floor, rested his head in his folded hands, and cried out. *Oh, Lord. What should I do? I've made such a mess of things. I should have been honest with Anna from the start, but you know as well as I do that she hasn't given me much chance to explain anything.*

A knock on the door interrupted his prayer, and he picked up the papers and tucked them under his pillow before answering. *"Jah?"*

His mother opened the door. "Is everything all right? *Datt* said you received some official-looking papers."

Simon handed his mother the documents, and after reading the letter, she moaned and sat beside him.

"Oh, dear. I'm certain it was hard for them to relinquish the care of their grandson. But this makes things much easier, *jah*?"

Simon dropped his chin. "I'm not sure."

Confused, Naomi asked, "What are you not sure of?"

"They gave me the option to put him up for adoption."

Naomi straightened her shoulders, took a breath, and breathed out. "You're not considering that?"

Simon stood and walked to the window. Once littered with stars, the night sky started to cloud over, much like his heart. "I'm not sure what's best, but how can I think of raising him alone?"

Naomi stood and rested her hands on her hips. "Simon Kauffman, you best think long and hard about what you deem necessary."

There was no mistaking his mother's disappointment by the way the door rattled as she closed it. Eli's words played over in his head as he watched the frozen ground beneath him take on a fresh layer of snow.

Suppose we wash ourselves only on the outside but never address the inside. In that case, we as Christians will never amount to anything but worldly, sinful people.

He was certain Eli's words were a message from God. Almost like a warning of sorts. For the last four years, he'd put his wants and desire before everything and everyone else in his life. And here again, he contemplated putting his desire to have Anna above his son's needs. He'd done everything right. He came home, put back on his Amish clothes, and sold everything that reminded him of his *Englisch* life. He even started attending an Amish church, praying, and staying in God's Word.

But had he ever addressed the selfishness of his own heart? Had he genuinely repented his past sins? He had given the situation over to God on more than one occasion. When the Lord started to answer his prayers, Simon wasn't sure he liked the answers. Especially if it meant Anna didn't come along as part of the package.

As if the devil gave him permission, the scenarios swirled around in his head like the smoke from his eldest *bruder's* farmhouse across the lane. If he signed the custody papers, he might lose Anna, but if he put him up for adoption, the boy would have two parents instead of one. And if that happened, and without Marcus adding to the problem, he might just have a chance to start over fresh with Anna. She may never find out about what he had done, and besides, they could have plenty of children of their own one day.

Distressed by his thoughts, he put the letters in his top dresser drawer and went to the barn to help with the evening milking.

***

Anna re-read Mr. Buckhannon's letter to be sure she understood it.

Anna,

It's not good news. The doctors have discovered inoperable tumors on Margaret's spine. We thought her back issues resulted from the car accident; we were unprepared for the aggressive cancer diagnosis. We are devastated, to say the least. This changes so many things, especially our ability to care for Steven.

I know this is a shock, but we are praying you will consider helping us with our grandson for a little longer.

We had our lawyer draw up a temporary guardianship for Steven in your name. This gives you complete control over his care until his biological father decides what his next step might be.

Until then, I have enclosed a check to cover his expenses and your payment for the next two months. That should give his father plenty of time to decide if he'll accept full custody or if he'd like us to continue the proceedings to place him up for adoption.

Anna stopped and read the last line over again. A deep ache settled in her chest at the thought of Steven being adopted.

Please pray his father will do what is right and accept responsibility for him. A son should be with his father.

As we discussed, we gave Steven's father a time limit to prove he could care for him. Even though we regret not allowing him the opportunity to have Steven when he asked, there is nothing we can do about it now. All we can do is wait for his reply and hope for the best. We pray he hasn't changed his mind.

Sincerely yours,

Neal Buckhannon

Anna folded the letter, tucked it back inside its envelope, made a little sympathetic clicking noise, and said aloud, "How terrible!"

Rebecca asked, "Problem?"

"Mrs. Buckhannon is not doing well. They want me to continue caring for Steven for a couple more months."

"Is that a problem?"

"I'm not sure, is it?"

"Oh, Anna, don't be silly. We love him being here, and he brings you so much joy. Eli and I were just commenting on how happy you are these days."

Anna reached over and kissed Steven's head as he sat in his highchair, chasing cereal over his tray. "I have taken quite a liking to the little guy."

"I'd say it's more than that. You are downright smitten."

Rebecca turned from the sink and dried her hands on a towel. "So, what now? What happens after two months?"

Anna knelt to pick up wayward cereal from the floor and answered, "Mr. Buckhannon mentioned that they had sent a letter to the boy's father asking him what he wanted them to do. They gave him the option for adoption or to take full custody."

Mary Ellen sat on the floor playing with a stack of plastic bowls, and Anna let Steven join her. "It sickens me to think he might have to go up for adoption. A child needs to be with his family. How will he ever know who he is or where he comes from?"

Anna sat at the table and rested her chin in her propped-up palm. "I can't help but think of Emma. Look how upset she was when she found out *Datt* and *Mamm* kept her identity a secret for so long. To live sixteen years thinking you were someone and then finding out you were not that person at all."

Rebecca sat down beside her and took a long sip of her tea. "*Jah*, it was hard on Emma, and it was hard on us too."

Anna exhaled. "I'm heart sick. Steven means the world to me, and I know you warned me about getting too attached." She paused and smiled at the children playing on the floor. "Just look at him. He's so happy and content. What if his father doesn't want him? I can hardly bear the thought of that."

"Now, Anna, you're putting the cart before the horse? You have no idea what's going on in the boy's father's life. Maybe he's not able to care for him. We have no idea what his life might look like. For all we know, he might not have the means to take care of him properly. Wouldn't it be wiser for him to go to a home with two parents?"

Anna stirred a long dollop of honey in her tea. "I suppose you're right, but it doesn't make it any easier to accept."

"Remember, *schwester*, you're just his nanny; you have no say in what his grandparents or, for that matter, his father decides to do."

Anna thought for a moment and excitedly cried, "I have an idea."

"*Jah?*"

"What if I write Steven's father a letter? Perhaps hearing how well-adjusted he is, how he sleeps through the night, and how he isn't a fussy baby might help him make the right decision."

Rebecca smiled and patted the back of Anna's hand. "I'm sure it wouldn't hurt, but you must realize that God already sees what's going to happen, and he doesn't need your help."

Anna pulled her arm away. "I know He doesn't need my help. But it won't hurt if Steven's father knows what a good baby he is."

A small giggle escaped Rebecca's lips. "If a letter will make you feel better, then there is stationary in the top drawer of the hutch."

***

After chores, Simon hooked up his buggy horse and headed to the Bricker farm for the day. He needed to speak to Eli, and maybe he'd catch a few words with Anna.

Big flakes gathered in his horse's mane as he passed Willow Creek. So many memories were made there with Anna that just driving through the covered bridge made his heart pause.

All night he struggled to understand God's plan. He knew he needed to have faith that God could see things that he couldn't, but when things weren't moving in the direction he planned, he felt himself giving up hope. Perhaps Eli would have some wise words. Maybe he'd help him understand things differently.

Simon pulled up beside the yarn shop and tethered his horse to the hitching post to the right of the porch. Smoke swirled from the small chimney, and without looking for Eli first, he followed the small imprints in the snow to the door.

A bell above the door clanged, and he heard Anna holler from the back room. "I'll be with you in a minute."

Simon brushed snow from his hat's wool brim and stood inside the door. A few tiny giggles made their way behind the curtain separating the workroom from the showroom. Marcus, balanced on Anna's hip, kicked his feet as she stepped from behind the room separator.

"Simon? Has your *mamm* gone through all that yarn already?"

"*Nee*. I'm here to see Eli. I thought I might stop in to talk to you for a few minutes first."

Anna sat Marcus on the floor and pulled a couple of empty yarn spools from the worktable for him to enjoy. Without taking her eyes off her ward, she asked, "What do you want to talk about?"

Simon shifted his weight, knelt to stack the wooden spools, and showed Marcus how to knock them over. Interested, Marcus crawled over closer. "Us?"

Anna sat on the stool and watched Marcus encourage Simon to stack them again. "Why are you in such a hurry? I've already told you I'm going to wait on God. Every time I take things into my own hands, I make a mess of things."

A heaviness in Simon's chest forced him to clench his teeth, and he leveled out his voice before he answered. "Please tell me what I must do to prove to you that I'm sorry and I've changed."

Anna waited and let silence fill the air before answering. "You don't have to prove anything to me. I must prove something to myself."

"What's that?"

"That I can wait on God and have faith He'll direct my steps when the time is right."

"But what if it's too late by then?"

Anna tilted her head in his direction. "Too late for what?"

Simon stood and squared his shoulders. "I don't know. Maybe us."

Anna shuffled a stack of pattern books. "Simon, you're not rushing me into anything. And besides, I'm not sure how I feel about you...or about us for that matter."

Letting out a breath, Simon asked, "How much time do you need?"

Anna shook her head. "Oh, Simon, you don't get it, do you?" Her voice cracked as she continued, "I was devastated when you left; I crumbled into a pitiful mess for years. It's only been the last few months since I've finally felt like I had a purpose in life other than waiting for you to make up your mind and return home. Now that the shoes are on the other foot, you aren't liking it much, are you?"

Simon dropped his shoulders and let her continue.

Anna paused before she affirmed. "There is no doubt that I still care for you, but I've been unable to figure out if I'm still romanticizing our courtship or truly have enough feelings left to build a future."

His eyes lifted, and he asked, "So there might be a future?"

"I didn't say that. All I'm saying is that a little part of my heart still has a place for you. Is that more than friendship? I don't know. Only God can see that through."

Simon put on his hat. "I suppose I understand that. Do I like it? *Nee*, but I understand. But I came back for one reason: to prove I could be trusted and still love you."

"Is that the only reason you returned?"

Simon struggled with telling her the truth, and he veered from being honest at the last moment. "You were the foremost reason."

She shook her head. "Then I'm afraid you came back for all the wrong reasons. I assumed you returned to find your way back to God, and if I was your only draw, then you need to go home and think about the condition of your heart."

Anna shook as she picked up Steven and pulled him close. "I have way too much to do caring for this child right now, and I don't have the time for this. Perhaps we can talk again when my nanny job is finished, but until then, I think we both have some healing to do."

Simon reached for the doorknob and started to say something but stopped before letting himself out.

Anna rested her chin on Steven's head and patted his back. "It's okay; Simon and I have some things to work out, that's all."

***

Simon took a deep breath and tipped his head against the heavy snowfall as he stepped off the porch. He was in no mood to seek Eli out. All he wanted to do was go home and find a place he could sulk in private.

In less than ten minutes, Anna shot down every hope he had about their future. Thoughts came racing through his head so fast he couldn't distinguish one from the next.

What did she know about the condition of his heart anyways? Was she any better by holding on to all his past mistakes? What did the Bible say about forgiveness? Maybe he needed to point that out to her.

She had no idea about his plans for their future home or the herb farm he wanted to build for her. And what would she think if she knew she cared for Cora's baby? I bet her holier than thou heart wouldn't be so kind, now would it? Life was easier when he didn't have to worry about caring for a child he had never planned.

CHAPTER 15

J acob sat with his head bowed. For weeks, an uneasiness surrounded him, almost like a warning he was about to face something much worse than his illness. At night, he would wake up, and the familiar feeling would return. What was God trying to show him? Was there something in his life He was trying to bring to his attention?

Wilma slid a plate of pancakes under his chin. "Please, Jacob, you need to eat. You've barely touched your food in weeks. You need your strength. Should I fix you a cup of Anna's tea again?"

"*Nee*, I'll eat." He picked up his fork and pushed the cold food around his plate. How could he explain the turmoil of feelings rushing through his head to his wife? Would she understand the pull he felt from God?

Wilma warmed his coffee. "What is it, Jacob? I wish you'd talk to me. I know something is eating away at you, and you've shut me out. Perhaps I can help you sort things out. Or we could take whatever it is to God and let him deal with it."

Jacob lifted his chin and sneered, "You don't think I've already done that?"

Wilma sunk into her chair. "How am I to know what you've done? You've barely said two words to me in weeks."

Jacob took a bite and thought. *She has no idea how hard it has been for me to walk away from my children. To shun them and turn them away. To give up my will and accept whatever I've been called to do. And now to hear promptings to go another direction entirely. How could that be from God? It must be my own will taking over my better judgment. It couldn't possibly be from Him. He certainly wouldn't assign me to one church and then put it on my heart to join another. It just wasn't right. It just couldn't be.*

While sipping his coffee, he remembered Bishop Weaver's words from the day he accepted the minister position for their Old Order Community. His friend, Mose Weaver, uttered a sentence that would be forever embedded in his memory. *It's a heavy burden that God has placed upon you this day, however, you can choose to make it one of your greatest job assignments. It's up to you. God has appointed you, but the responsibility lays in your hands, not God's alone. What you choose to make of it is yours alone. Will you decide to make it a joy or a burden?*

Chosen by lot, appointed by God, he promised to visit the fatherless and widows, help the sick and needy, and admonish sinners. But more than anything, to be a shining example of the gospel. Had he been that to his children and to the members of his *g'may*?

He pushed his plate away. "I'm just not hungry. I'm sorry you went through all this trouble. Keep my plate on the stove to warm. I may come back for it."

A cloud of mist filled his wife's eyes. "Sure. I'll do whatever you wish."

Jacob reached for her hand. "Wilma, I'm sorry. I know these last couple of months haven't been easy on you. I have a lot on my mind these days, and I just need some time to figure a few things out."

He slid his chair back and stood as if trying to find his words. "Stella had an *Englisch* Bible on her nightstand when she died. I looked for it this morning, and it wasn't where I thought it might be. Have you seen it?"

Wilma went to the cupboard near the back door, pulled a small step stool over to the counter, and removed the book from the top shelf.

Before handing it to him, she reached for his hand. "I pray you find the answers you're searching for."

Jacob nodded and retreated to the living room. Something happened during his illness that he couldn't quite explain. It was like a longing overtook him, and he couldn't stop living in the past. At every turn, he heard Stella's voice as loud as if she was still living.

In the dark of the night, with Wilma lying beside him, Stella visited him in his dreams. Their last few moments were so vivid in the hours right before dawn that the pain of losing her was heavy on his chest when he awoke.

Her last plea was for him to seek Jesus and to make sure all their children and grandchildren knew the truth of the Bible. She begged him to read the *Englisch* Bible and understand what Jesus taught about salvation. At the time, he didn't know why she felt it necessary, but he granted her the last wish, at least in words. And then life happened, and he'd forgotten his promise.

Only after Anna had nursed him back to life did Stella's words become louder. Not even after all four of his children left the church was her voice as clear. She cried out to him in the dark, reminding him of his promise.

Just that morning, he woke with tears on his pillow as Stella's last words hovered in the darkness. *Promise me, Jacob, I'll see you in heaven.* After coming close to death himself, her words haunted him to a point he'd been questioning everything he'd ever stood for.

Wilma stood over his chair with a fresh cup of coffee. "I warmed it back up for you."

"Denki," he muttered and pointed to the side table.

Wilma turned to leave, and Jacob asked, "Why did you allow Anna in when I was sick?"

His once surefooted wife lowered her head. "I prayed for help, and Anna knocked on the door within minutes."

He mumbled, "Coincidence."

Wilma stood in silence and let his word sink in before responding. *"Nee,* an answered prayer."

She slipped in her boots near the front door and wrapped a shawl around her shoulders. "I'm getting the mail."

A gust of wind blew around his chair with the opened door, and he watched Wilma, out the window, shuffle toward the mailbox.

Wilma had changed over the last couple of months. Maybe it was his brush with death, or perhaps she was tired after all they had been through. Whatever it was, she was quieter and more reserved than ever before. He found himself comparing her to Stella and half enjoyed the change.

Regret and guilt covered him, like the scarf Wilma tied around her chin. When he married Stella, it was for love and nothing else but to serve the Lord the best way he knew.

He never dreamed he would marry again. However, when it came time for the ordination of new ministers, he knew his only chance to be considered would be to take a wife. Jacob would be the first to admit those first few months with Wilma were difficult.

Never having children of her own, she didn't understand the family dynamics, especially regarding adult children. Let alone the challenges they faced when their community split.

When she opened the door, a whirl of snow followed her, and she assured, "No doubt about having a white Christmas this year." She handed Jacob the stack of mail and slipped out of her boots.

Jacob sifted through the stack of seed catalogs. He unfolded the Budget newspaper, releasing a letter to the floor. Wilma bent to pick it up and read the name neatly printed in the upper left-hand corner. "Emma Yoder?"

Jacob scoffed. "She could have left it on the porch. What a waste of a stamp." Wilma hung her coat and scarf on the peg by the door and headed to the kitchen.

Before releasing the flap, Jacob held his daughter's letter in his hand. For over twenty years of Emma's life, Jacob and she had been inseparable. A pang of remorse lodged in his throat at all he missed with his youngest child. Emma and Samuel lived less than half a mile down the road. But as far as their two communities split, she might as well live in Willow Brook, ten miles away. Pushing regret from his mind, he read her letter.

Dear Datt,

This letter is long overdue, but I must try once more to plead with you on behalf of your children and the grandchildren you barely know. Too much time has passed, and I have missed you so much during our separation.

Like every day in the past two years, life has gone on without much regard for the Byler family. We work, bake, take care of animals, and raise our families like our ancestors have done for centuries without regard for the hardships laid before us. I never dreamed of facing the future without you in it.

But I've wept instead when I've needed to talk to you. Even to sit in your presence, but again I'm unable to express the yearnings of my heart.

I know God has a plan and a purpose for all He does. A master plan I can't even begin to comprehend. And I know He doesn't ask me to understand, only to believe, trust, and submit to His will. I'm sure in His own time, He will explain, perhaps more importantly, when I'm truly ready.

However, in the meantime, He laid it on my heart to reach out to you one last time. I wanted to come to visit with you in person, but after you chased Anna away, I didn't want to upset you more. And to do so would have been wrong according to the shunning.

Lately, I am reminded of something you once told me while going through the challenges of my teenage years. You said to me that God does not want to make our problems smaller to make them bearable. But He wants us to let his grace become greater to make the task possible. That's where I find myself today. Praying that I will accept the job he has put before me. The mission of living so close but still so far away from you.

Datt, I beg you to reconsider this separation. I know Mamm shared her newfound love for Jesus before she died. I also know she made sure each of us children knew the truth regarding trusting our salvation through Christ and not through a set of rules and regulations meant to scare us into obedience.

I understand you've been put in a tough spot to follow the ruling of the Old Order, but please, Datt, open the Bible and read for yourself. The men of the New Order Fellowship are not wrong in their interpretation. Jesus gives us two things to follow. Love your neighbor as you love yourself, and no one comes to the Lord except through Him.

I don't know about you, but I want to be with Mamm and James in heaven one day, and the only way I will do that is through Christ. Not by how well I followed the rules of the Ordnung.

I'll leave you with this last thought…

The ties in a family are often formed by the challenges they face together. Please, Datt, I know we have not always agreed on everything, but I hope we agree that we need to share the burden of life together as one.

God gives us only one family and precisely puts us exactly where we need to be to bring him the most glory.

Your loving daughter, Emma

P.S. The Lord has granted Samuel and I a second chance at parenthood come this spring.

Jacob folded the letter on his lap and stared out the window. He relied on a living hope for his salvation all his life. One that was orchestrated by how well he followed the rules and what kind of person he was, believing his deeds would favor him with God.

Now, what his children and his deceased wife proposed was something he couldn't fathom. How can one trust in Jesus to secure salvation? This notion was the same thing that forced the ex-communication on his children. To accept this as truth would lead him down the same path.

As he closed his eyes to lift a heartfelt prayer, Jacob heard Stella's voice whispering, *"Just say, 'Jesus.'"*

***

Emma donned a wrap and slipped out the side door into the clear, cold winter air. Carrying a plastic container full of peanut butter cookies, she braced herself for the mile walk to

Rebecca's. According to Samuel, a surprise visit with her *schwester's* is precisely what she needed.

She still prayed the letter she'd sent to her *datt* three days earlier would make a difference. Agonizing over the words for hours, she hoped they would convey her heartfelt plea. She told Samuel she would never stop trying, even if the letter said it was her last try.

The scraping of metal wheels on the snow-packed road made Emma move off to the side. The buggy slowed as it passed and stopped a few yards ahead. When she made her way to its side, the canvas covering had been unsnapped, and Wilma sat waiting.

Emma struggled against the resentment rising up in her, the hurt and betrayal at her stepmother's hand laid heavy on her chest. If it wasn't for Anna's reassuring words about how Wilma treated her during their father's illness, Emma might have turned away.

"I want to explain a few things…" Wilma's voice cracked.

The expression on Emma's face must have unleashed a warning because Wilma pleaded. "Please hear me out."

Wilma blinked and stared into the mounting snow. "Are you headed to Rebecca's?"

"*Jah.*"

"Please get in out of the snow."

Emma pulled her coat tighter, but the cold still seeped in. Not so much from the temperature, but from the icy reception Wilma had always given her.

Shame filled Emma as she tried to find a way to graciously decline her invitation. *Honor thy father and mother...*rang loudly in her head, so she climbed into Wilma's buggy. *Oh, Jesus, forgive me. What sort of witness am I of your love if all I can think of is all the wrong, she has caused this family?* Folding her hands on her lap, she prayed, *Let me be your light.*

Suddenly calm inside, Emma knew what to do...*listen.*

Wilma snapped the reins and pulled back out to the center of the road. "Emma, I know we didn't have the time to get to know one another like we should have. And that is no fault of yours. I take full responsibility for my shortcomings."

Wilma let out a shuddering breath. "I waited so long to marry. When it finally happened, I was jealous of your *datt's* relationship with his children, especially you."

Her face was white, her expression concerning. "I wanted him all to myself." The steady clip-clop hung in the air as Wilma continued. "I poisoned your father against you all."

Emma filled with sorrow at her confession. "Wilma, you didn't poison him against us. We know *Datt* loves us. He turned his back on us because we left the church, which had nothing to do with you. That was our decision."

Shame etched Wilma's face. "But you don't know how hard I've worked to keep you separated and this community divided."

"I find it hard to believe your one voice had anything to do with it."

"Oh, Emma, you underestimate me. I've had a lifetime to hone my craft of stirring up trouble. If I want something bad enough, I'll do almost anything to make it happen."

Emma stopped and began to realize things through Wilma's eyes and asked, "But why?"

"If I encouraged Jacob to uphold his position, I didn't have to fear he'd push me out of his life in exchange for his children. As long as he was a minister, I was accepted. Even though I knew it was wrong to live a lie."

"Wilma, this doesn't have anything to do with his position. It has to do with the condition of his heart. We want you and *Datt* to know the truth and live by it. As followers of Jesus, it's not our job to save you. Only God can do that. But it's our job to show you the way."

Wilma started to cry as she pulled into Rebecca's driveway. "But you don't understand. If I kept him focused on the behavior-oriented path toward pleasing God, he wouldn't want to look into the inward transformation he was seeing in his children."

Emma let out a small gasp. "You know!"

Wilma pulled the buggy to a stop. "Oh, Emma, I know more than you think, and I fully understand what your church stands for."

"I'm so confused."

Wilma took a few seconds to respond and kept her eyes straight ahead when she spoke. "I'm ashamed to confess, but I can't hide behind a curtain of lies any longer. Emma, please understand, that when your father asked me to be his wife, it was my answer to a lifelong dream. I said yes before I realized his church still followed the rules and expectations that promised God's acceptance in return for their human effort."

"But you married him anyway?"

"I had reservations. I felt I could follow him even though I knew I was encouraging your father to be pridefully focused on his good works even though I knew it to be wrong."

Emma shook her head. "Do you believe Jesus is your answer to salvation?"

Wilma wrapped the reins around the knob and folded her hands on her lap. After waiting a few seconds, she replied, "I do, but I've come to realize I'm no better than the Pharisees in the Old Testament. They would honor God with their lips, but their heart was far from Him." Wilma paused and continued with a crack in her voice. "I know God hates the outward show, and I've lied to Jacob and myself in thinking I could continue this way."

Emma turned in her seat. "Admitting the wrong is half the battle. You know all you have to do is repent, and you can make it right?"

"I know, and I have. Confessing the part I played in all of this is part of that repentance."

Emma took off her glove and rubbed her forehead. "It's so much to take in."

"That's not all." Wilma paused. "In the beginning, I thought I could save him, and I prayed that God would open his eyes to see the truth. I believed that if I continued to petition God on his behalf and be a supportive wife, there would come a time I could speak to him about the truth. I…I knew we weren't equally yoked…but I wanted to be married so badly."

Wilma pulled her coat tighter. "After a while, I came to enjoy the status of being a minister's wife. The women in the community looked up to me. I didn't have that in my old *g'may*. And…and then I became jealous of you children."

"Oh, Wilma, you need to tell *Datt* all this."

"I'm certain your father is already figuring much of this out himself. God is already working on his heart; I can feel it."

Emma laid her hand across Wilma's arm. "You think so?"

"I do. He asked for your mother's Bible this morning, so I've decided to wait to see what happens. I want him to come to this on his own, without prompting and prodding from me. If he asks, I will certainly tell him that the gospel offers life-giving, life-transformation through the gift of salvation. But he has to realize that for himself."

"Oh, Wilma, I pray you're right. Wouldn't it be wonderful if our families could be restored?"

"Emma, I don't want you to get your hopes up too much. It's going to take a lot for him to leave a rule-following group where they believe that their behavior and beliefs are right and everyone else is wrong. He doesn't know any other way."

Emma smiled. "But he does know; I'm sure *Mamm* shared it with him, just like she did all of us."

Emma reached out and squeezed her stepmother's gloved hand. "Please come inside. It's time you got to know your grandchildren, and Anna and Rebecca need to hear all this."

***

Jacob waited until Wilma pulled away from the barn before opening Stella's Bible. A wave of emotion stung his nose as he ran his thumb over the thin pages. During the last few days of Stella's life, she insisted the *Englisch* Bible stayed tucked at her side.

As he sifted through the chapters, a small slip of pink paper stopped his thumb. A single verse in Stella's dainty handwriting, and his name stared back at him.

Luke 23:43 – Jacob

Jacob turned to the Gospel of Luke and read the verse aloud. *"Truly, I tell you, today you will be with me in paradise."*

Stella's dying words came to his mind again, and he tried to make sense of her message and the scripture. Re-reading the entire scripture about the crucifixion of Jesus, he laid back in the chair and asked, "Lord, what are you trying to show me?"

He closed his eyes, played the scene in his head, and thought. *The men who hung on either side of Jesus that day were thieves. Naked and alone, doomed to suffer for their sins on the cross without any hope for the future.*

One man hurled insults at Jesus, and the other rebuked him. The first thief asked Jesus to remember him when he entered his kingdom, and Jesus replied, "Truly, I tell you, today you will be with me in paradise."

Jacob opened his eyes and closed the Bible. As he wandered to the window, he thought. *That sinner didn't follow any rules. He wasn't even dressed in fine clothes; he was naked. What did he have to offer Jesus? He had no proof of his good works. He had nothing to give him but his belief.*

A letter he received from Matthew came to mind. A frantic search through a stack of papers on his desk revealed Matthew's plea.

Datt,

I know you struggle with understanding my decision to leave the Old Order, and I pray it will become clear one day. Until then, I wanted to share a few truths I've discovered.

First, we cannot earn God's acceptance by observing a set of rules and traditions. Not even the most religious, hardworking, and faithful person will be good enough to get to heaven without going through Jesus first.

Second, the purpose of the Old Testament's law was to show us we needed a savior. Not one of us can say we haven't broken one of the Ten Commandments. The law shows us we aren't good enough and need help.

And lastly, righteousness from God comes from faith in Christ alone to all those who believe in him.

Sarah and I will continue to pray for you.

Matthew

When Jacob received the letter more than a year ago, he tucked it away, giving it no more than a passing thought. But as he re-read the words, the thief on the cross came to mind. That sinner had nothing to prove to Jesus but his faith.

Jacob sunk down in a chair, buried his face in his hands and prayed. Oh, Jesus, help me have faith like that thief. *Lord, here*

I am. I have nothing good to offer, other than from this moment forward, I believe you are who you say you are. Please forgive me for all the years I've trusted in my own flesh to enter the kingdom of heaven. I can't believe I've wasted all these years. Please take me as a sinner of false hope and make me whole. Amen.

CHAPTER 16

It had been three weeks since Anna had heard from the Buckhannon's. Christmas had come and gone, and any hope of Steven's father coming to claim him vanished.

"You look tired, Anna," said Rebecca, as she passed. "You look like you're bearing the world's weight on your shoulders."

"*Jah*, I haven't slept well the last few nights," Anna admitted.

"I would think you would be as happy as me after *Datt* and Wilma showed up to church on Sunday."

"I'm pleased about that, don't get me wrong." Her eyes brimmed with tears and her voice trembled. "It's just that I fear for Steven. I hoped his father would have come for him by now. I'm afraid he's decided to put him up for adoption."

Steven toddled out from under the table and pulled himself up on Anna's lap. "If only he'd come to meet the little guy before he decided."

"Now, don't go and get yourself all worked up. You don't know anything for sure." Rebecca wiped John Paul's nose and asked, "Did you ever write that letter you mentioned?"

Anna picked Steven up and checked his diaper. "I started to, but then I got pulled away for some reason and never finished it."

"Perhaps it would help. His father doesn't even know him. At first, I didn't think it a good idea, but it might be your letter will show him what he's missing."

***

Simon kept his head hung low as he made his way to a seat on the wooden bench in the Yoder's living room, where church was being held that day. For weeks, he'd thrown himself into work in hopes of it drowning out the turmoil his conscience experienced. Even the sympathetic silence he'd received from his parents the last few days was deafening.

As he waited for the rest of the younger men to file in, he lifted his head high enough to locate Anna. Her starched white *kapp,* which laid slightly askew from Marcus pulling on her strings, swayed when she pushed the child's hand away. Propping him over her shoulder, Marcus caught Simon's form and muttered something in words only another baby would understand.

Anna turned in her seat and followed the child's outstretched hand. With little more than a recollection nod, Anna pulled the child to her lap and faced the front of the room.

Simon struggled to understand how his heart could be so wound up in things he obviously couldn't have. Was it punishment for all the pain he caused both Anna and his family over the years? Perhaps it was God's punishment for walking away from his faith and leaving Anna. He even asked his father if he felt the Lord would withhold the longings of his heart for past mistakes.

His father's words were little comfort as he explained God doesn't punish us because Jesus took that for us on the cross. But the Bible did say bad things can happen due to God's discipline. They are not a punishment for sin; instead, they are a correction, much like a parent would correct a child.

His mind and heart constantly battled over wanting Anna and doing the right thing for Steven Marcus. To have one meant giving up the other. What should he choose? He'd kept his secret too long for Anna to trust him again.

Simon mouthed the words to the chant-like songs that his friends and family sang around him, giving little thought to the meanings. He couldn't help but feel like a failure in everything he'd tried to do.

Surrounded by men who had taken a stand against their Old Order's teachings, he felt inferior to their strong faith. He was nothing but a liar. He said all the right things, dressed in the right clothes, and faithfully attended church every other Sunday. But was his heart right with God? Did he really understand his character?

The more he sat and tried to listen to Minister Yoder's teachings, the more he felt suffocated by his conflicted yearnings. Had all his prayers and confessions fallen on deaf ears? If his God was all he said He was, wouldn't He answer his prayers? Distressed by his doubts, he quietly slipped out the back door.

A burst of cold air burned Simon's lungs as he followed the path alongside Yoder's Strawberry acres to Willow Creek. The sun glistened through the frozen trees, and he pulled his waistcoat tighter and buried his hands in his pockets.

He sauntered to the spot where he and Anna had discovered their love for each other so many years earlier. He longed to roam through the woods, to sit on a log, and listen to the ripples swishing over the rocks. Life was so much simpler then.

He sat on a frozen overturned log, exhausted and quiet, waiting patiently for some form of reassurance. A sudden peace overcame him where a storm had been raging for weeks, and he prayed, *Forgive me. I keep stumbling, and I seem to keep losing my way. I want to do what is right, even though it means pain and sacrifice. Lord, make your will, my will, and help me accept it without question.*

After a while, he arose, opened his eyes against the bitter wind, and felt peace. He knew what he must do.

***

Naomi sifted through the stack of mail, and her heart leaped at the letter addressed to Simon. The familiar return address of Buckhannons' lawyer set off an array of emotions she tried to settle before returning to the house. She knew Simon struggled with accepting what he must do, and she prayed he would make the right choice for the sake of her grandson.

No matter how old her sons were, their challenges seemed to grow greater the older they became. As children, it was easy to put a band-aid on things and send them on their way with a cookie in hand.

However, now their struggles sent her to her knees more than ever. Her chest ached in the hollow of her heart for them to choose the Lord over their human desires. Her constant prayer was that they would humbly accept their path.

It was harder now than ever to be a parent of adult children. Their wise counsel fell on deaf ears most times, and she and Jebediah both had to stand back and silently watch. Jebediah often reminded her the best thing they could do was petition God on their behalf.

As she entered the warmth of her kitchen, Simon sat at his place at the table, sipping a cup of coffee. Naomi hung her coat, unwrapped the blue headscarf she had tied under her chin, and said, "There is a letter from the Buckhannon's."

Simon pulled the official-looking envelope from the stack and slid his finger under the sealed flap.

After a quick note from the lawyer, he laid the message aside and unfolded the handwritten letter.

To Steven's father,

I know you don't know me, but I am Anna Byler, the nanny Mr. and Mrs. Buckhannon hired to care for your son. It has come to my attention that you may consider putting your son up for adoption. I pray that you will prayerfully take heed to my words.

Your son, Steven, is an energetic and thriving eleven-month-old. His dark curly hair and brown eyes sparkle as he meets each new day. Once prone to tantrums, your son has become a joyful child.

As he grows, I see more and more of his determination to figure things out on his own. He is curious and loves exploring his surroundings, but don't all boys? He has a zeal for life and plays peacefully with my sister's children.

You may not be aware of my Amish upbringing, but I was raised in a culture where God, family, and community are at the core of our being. I pray that whatever your background may be; you have a strong faith and will dig deep into your understanding and do what is best for Steven.

Considering that, I beg you to ponder how Steven needs to know where he comes from and who his family is. I am so afraid that he'll never understand those things if you put him up for adoption. Children need to be surrounded by family, and I am heartbroken to think he won't know you.

I am confident the Buckhannons' will interview and choose a family best suited for Master Steven, should you decide on that path. Still, I wouldn't be able to forgive myself if I didn't at least try to help you see who your son is and how badly he needs you. A strong-willed child needs a strong father; from how his grandparents described you, you carry those qualities.

I understand you may feel you can't raise a child on your own, but I must believe one father's love can be sufficient if it comes from the heart.

I must trust in the judgment of Mr. and Mrs. Buckhannon, and they tell me you come from a strong family who will support you in all things. In times like these, we must put our desires aside and do what is right in the eyes of God...even if it goes against our hearts.

I will continue to pray for both you and Steven.

Sincerely,

Anna Byler

Simon's heart pounded so hard he could scarcely place the letter back in the tight envelope. Without a word, he carried the letter to his room and put it in the spot where his signed document once lay just that morning. Before dawn, he placed his decision in the mailbox, leaving his son's fate in the recipient's hands.

***

Naomi held her breath until Simon's footsteps made their way back to the kitchen and watched as he carried his empty cup to the sink. Hesitant to break the silence, she declared, "Whatever it is, don't let it still your peace. You've made your decision, and you must live with it."

Simon stood and stared out over the frozen landscape of his family's home and mumbled, "This is the hardest thing I've ever had to do."

Her son's pain, so clearly etched on his young face, spoke of great sacrifice in doing what he felt was best for Steven Marcus. She lifted a silent prayer on his behalf that God would show him Grace and understanding in accepting his choices. Shifting her weight to accommodate her aging knees, she said, "This is surely a matter to be prayed about. God will prevail; he always does."

Without turning his gaze, he retorted, "Please pray I don't wallow in this season long."

CHAPTER 17

The days flew by that week in anticipation of Mr. Buckhannon's planned visit. A letter had come earlier in the week stating that he would be driving through Willow Springs on his way back to Atlanta and wanted to stop by and see Steven.

She hoped Neal would notice how much Steven had grown and how he seemed happy and content in his surroundings. There was no doubt he had grown so much that she had to sew him a dark pair of trousers and a small light blue shirt to match the style of the other children in the community.

On the outside, he blended into his surroundings and had become a constant member of the Bricker household. She wondered if Neal would reject her choice of clothes for the child.

The sound of tires on the frozen driveway alerted her attention to his arrival. Wiping a smudge of leftover oatmeal off Steven's face, Anna headed to the door, balancing the child on her hip.

When she opened the door, Mr. Buckhannon had already made it up the front steps. "Welcome, please come in out of the cold," Anna said as she stood aside, letting Neal step into the warmth of the living room.

A genuine smile encased the older man's face as he reached out and held Steven's tiny fingers. "Look at you! You've grown so much in just a few months. I hardly recognize you." Neal poked Steven's belly. "Miss Anna hasn't had trouble getting you to eat."

Anna pushed his shirt into the waistband of his little pants. "Eating is no longer an issue for sure and certain."

Mr. Buckhannon wiped his feet on the blue and yellow braided rug at the door and took off his jacket. "I had some business to take care of in the area and had to stop and visit with you both."

Anna pointed to the pair of rockers under the front window. "Do you want to sit for a spell? I made fresh coffee and baked a batch of cinnamon rolls this morning."

Neal found a seat. "That sounds wonderful. I've missed your baking. The hospital food is anything but appealing these days."

Anna stopped and asked, "How is Margaret?"

Neal's tone turned serious. "As well as expected, I guess. She's in a lot of pain, and they keep her heavily medicated most days. I had to come home long enough to take care of some business, but when I get back, I'll need to start the process of moving her to a care facility. The hospital's done all they can do for her now."

"I'm so sorry. I know she was hoping to get back on her feet again."

Neal handed Steven a toy. "I'm afraid all we can do now is keep her comfortable. I've realized it's only a matter of time now. The cancer continues to spread, and at the rate it's growing, it's just a matter of time."

Anna shook her head and moved toward the kitchen. As she made a tray to carry in the front room, her thoughts made her chest heavy. Thinking about how Steven wouldn't remember his grandmother weighed on her and reminded her that her mother never had the chance to meet any of her grandchildren.

After setting the tray on the stand between the two rockers, Mr. Buckhannon took one of the filled cups and sat back in his chair. "Anna, I can't thank you enough for taking such good care of our grandson. It was refreshing to know he was well cared for, and I didn't need to worry."

Anna crossed her legs and took a sip of her sweetened coffee. "It's what you hired me for, and it was more of a joy for me than a job. Honestly, I'm not sure what I'll do when the little guy leaves."

Mr. Buckhannon's face turned solemn. "I'm afraid that will happen soon. I met with our lawyer the other day, and he drew up the final paperwork, and I delivered it to his father this morning."

"What did the father decide?"

"That is good news. His father has asked to have full custody."

Anna relaxed in her chair. "Oh, thank goodness. I've been praying he would make that decision. Steven needs to know his father and where he comes from."

Her stomach flipped slightly when she realized she would no longer be needed to care for the child she so fondly fell for. "When…when will he come for him?"

"That is what I came to tell you. If it suits you, he'd like to come this afternoon."

"Today?" Anna's voice cracked.

"Two o'clock, to be exact."

Neal watched as the young girl processed the timing. After visiting with Simon that morning, he figured out she and Simon had not reconciled, and Simon would be raising the boy on his own. He wished he could persuade Anna to give the young man another chance. However, after learning Simon had yet to confess to being his father, he felt it best to let it rest. He trusted things would work themselves out if it was in God's plan. Besides, everything would come out in the open soon enough.

Neal raised an eyebrow and asked, "What will you do next?"

Anna sat her cup down and leaned back in her chair. "I guess I really don't know. I suppose I'll return to helping my *schwester* in the yarn shop."

"By your tone, it doesn't sound like something you'll enjoy."

"*Jah.*"

"You're so good with Steven; perhaps I could help you secure another nanny position."

"I've thought of that. But I'm not sure I can do that again. I'm going to miss him so."

A slight upward grin settled on Neal's lips. "Perhaps you'll not miss him as much as you think?"

"Ohhh…I'm certain of it. I've grown quite attached to him."

"I can see that, and I'm sure he'll miss you too. I'm just saying you might be able to set something up with his father where you could still be part of his life. He is a single father, so he might need an extra set of hands. Especially in the beginning when he needs to get accustomed to his schedule and all."

Anna wrapped her arms across her chest and pondered Mr. Buckhannon's suggestion. "You mentioned he comes from a close family, so I'm certain they won't need my help."

Neal smiled. "I wouldn't be so sure of that."

"We'll see. I'll offer my help and let his father decide."

Mr. Buckhannon stood. "Anna, I can't thank you enough for all you've done to help us out, and if I can do anything to help you find another assignment, call me."

Neal knelt and kissed Steven on the top of his head. "You, my little guy, I'll see soon. Your father knows how much it will mean to me to stay in your life and has agreed to keep me involved."

Anna's eyes lit up. "That's wonderful news. Steven needs to know his grandfather."

Anna walked the older gentleman to the door and let him engulf her in a hug. While the endearment was mostly an

Englisch tradition, she felt comfortable in the grandfatherly affection. As Steven crawled to her side, she picked him up and waited until Mr. Buckhannon pulled away before shutting the door.

Only after she was alone with Steven did she allow a set of tears to release to her cheeks. She never dreamed it would be so hard to let him go. To abruptly stop caring for him and release him to the unknown. Would his father know how to calm him in the night? Would he be aware of his tendency to put every little thing he found on the floor in his mouth? What about his tender tummy resistance to cow's milk?

Placing the child on the floor, she retrieved a pad and pen out of the drawer and started writing down Steven's likes and dislikes and his sleep and nap schedule. The thought of him waking up in a strange room made her anxious, and she wondered if she should suggest she come help him adjust to his new surroundings.

At every hour, the clock rang, and Anna cringed at the finality of it all. Eli and Rebecca took the children to her father's so Eli could help her *datt* with a project in the woodshop. She couldn't help but be joyful at the door that had been opened concerning her father but devastated at another closing before her eyes.

Anna gathered all of Steven's things and placed them in two boxes near the front door. After a short nap and a fresh set of clothes, they sat on the floor playing with wooden blocks shortly before two.

The knock on the door alarmed her, and she peered out the window, surprised at the horse and buggy tethered to the post near the front of Eli's porch.

She couldn't see the visitor from where she sat and was instantly annoyed at the impromptu visitor. It wasn't a good time, with Steven's father due any minute.

Patting the top of Steven's head, she moved toward the door. A burst of cold entered the room as soon as her eyes fell on Simon's form. Looking around him, she said, "Simon, this isn't a good time. I'm expecting someone."

Tucking his chin to the wind swirling around the house, he asked, "May I come in?"

Again, Anna looked down the driveway and back toward Steven. He was playing on the floor, oblivious to the change about to take place. "For a minute, I suppose. At least to keep the cold out."

Simon stepped inside and removed his hat. Without moving off the rug, he stepped out of his boots.

Her mouth became dry, and she found it hard to speak when she took notice of his intended stay, Anna stiffened. "Simon, this really isn't a good time."

Simon's chest beat so hard, he was sure Anna could hear it from where she settled back on the floor next to his son. The muscle in his jaw tensed, and he swallowed hard. "Anna, I'm the visitor you're expecting."

"How can that be? I didn't even know you were coming."

"You did. I know Mr. Buckhannon was here this morning and told you of my arrival."

As if in slow motion, Anna looked to Simon and back to Steven. The curls that had flipped up at the back of Simon's head mimicked the tight curls covering Steven's head. The shape of his chin and bridge of his nose matched the man staring back at her.

A wave of nausea and pain at Simon's confession left her speechless. Steven crawled to Simon's side and held his hands up to him. Accommodating his son's request, Simon pulled him close and waited for her response. The uncanny way the child felt at ease with Simon left her knowing what he said was true.

"I…I tried to tell you multiple times, but I never could quite find the words." He paused long enough to let her absorb it all. "Please, Anna, say…something…anything."

She handed him Steven's jacket. "I wrote out his schedule along with his likes and dislikes. I tucked it in the side of that box."

Simon nodded and sat down in the rocker to balance Steven Marcus on his knee to put on his coat.

An eerie quiet surrounded them as they both struggled to make sense of the unfamiliar territory. "Anna, he's going to miss you. Please tell me you will help us make this transition easy."

Anna walked to the door, held it open, and took the child from his arms as he carried the boxes to the buggy. When all of Steven's belongings were tucked safely in the back of the carriage, Simon held his hands out to accept his son.

Anna released her hold on Steven and fought to control the tears teetering her bottom lashes. "You won't need my help. Your *mamm* is plenty capable of helping you navigate through parenthood."

The sting of her words took on a new level of discouragement. "Perhaps so, but I was hoping you'd agree to let me turn to you."

Anna remained still, trying to comprehend all he was asking. The pain of knowing he failed to be honest sent her spiraling into the depths of despair. In just a few minutes, all the progress she'd made to control her anxiety and offer Simon forgiveness resurfaced in an ugly place of bitterness.

When Steven wiggled and turned toward Anna with outstretched arms, she stepped back into the house and closed the door. Only after hearing Simon's footsteps descend the porch did she allow herself to breathe. Leaning back against the door, she slid to the floor, burying her head in her hands.

***

For the rest of the afternoon, Anna tried to busy herself with meaningless tasks until Eli, Rebecca, and the *kinner* returned home. As soon as Mary Ellen had removed her winter wear, she ran to the front room, calling Steven's name. The emptiness returned as her *schwester* explained things to her daughter. As resilient as children were, Mary Ellen accepted the change and went on about her play.

Rebecca laid her hand on Anna's shoulder. "It must have been harder on you than you imagined."

Anna wiped her nose on the wrinkled-up hankie she held in her hands. "You have no idea. It was far worse than I ever dreamed."

"Oh, Anna, what can I do for you? I was afraid you were getting way too attached to him."

Anna couldn't control the long hiccup sob as she tried to speak. Tenderly Rebecca pulled her close and let her rest her head on her shoulder. "It...it's...not...that. It's...Si...mon.

"Simon? I'm confused. Did Simon visit today?" Rebecca hugged her tighter. "Oh, you poor child. Of all days for Simon to stop by."

A shudder of deep-throated cries shook Anna's tiny frame, which Rebecca tried to soothe by whispering comforting words in her ear. When the last of the moans subsided, Anna pulled away and wiped her face, and blew her nose. Allowing time for Rebecca to question her. "What did Simon say that has upset you so?"

"He's Steven's father."

"What? How can that be?"

Anna rubbed her eyes with the palm of her hands. "All this time, he let me care for Steven and never told me he was his?"

In shock at Anna's explanation, Rebecca stayed quiet and let her continue. "I should have put two and two together. Steven took to him easily, and they favored each other. Why didn't I see it? I feel like such a fool."

"Oh, Anna, why do you feel foolish?"

Anna raised her voice slightly. "Don't you see? I gave my heart to two Kaufmann boys, and I can't have either."

Rebecca reached for the box of tissues and handed them to her *schwester*. "Who says you can't have them?"

Anna didn't answer but blew her nose and glared at Rebecca.

"Now, don't give me that look. I think you're too upset to see the big picture. I see God's hands all over this. How on earth did you, just by coincidence, answer an ad to care for Simon's child?"

"Oh, Rebecca, I miss him so!" she exclaimed suddenly. "The pain almost tears my heart in two. How will I ever live knowing that my little Steven is so close but still so far away?"

"I'm not entirely sure, but I know where you can find comfort."

"*Jah.*"

"And I can't help but think this is all in God's plan. Maybe once the shock of it wears off, you can stand back and see what the Lord is trying to teach you."

"I know you're right, and please remind me I need to concentrate on the blessing He gave me by allowing me to care for Steven, if only for a short while. But I'm still inclined to want my own way. And my inner will wants to be mad at Simon for letting me down again. It's like he left me all over again."

"Anna, you just need to get over that. You've been carrying around this resentment toward Simon for too long. I can't help but think it's half the reason why you struggled with anxiety for so many years."

Anna stood to set the table as Rebecca started supper. "Caring for Steven helped me through much of that. I honestly haven't felt that underlying edge of worry in the last few months. Maybe being busy helped me through the worst of it."

Rebecca added hamburger to a hot skillet and added, "I think the power of love is stronger than fear. When you were busy loving and caring for Steven, there was no room for your fear or anxiety to take root."

Anna pulled a stack of plates from the cupboard. "I must admit, I'm afraid of what will happen now. I don't want to lose myself in that self-pity again; to be quite honest, it's exactly what I've done all afternoon. The thought of being around Simon and Steven makes my pulse race."

Rebecca turned from the stove and said, "God didn't promise to keep us from trials; rather, He promised to use our trials for our good and His glory."

Anna filled Mary Ellen's sippy cup with water. "I trust in God's promises, really I do."

"Then you have nothing to worry about, *jah*?" Rebecca asked as she stirred in leftover potatoes, carrots, and a quart of stewed tomatoes into the cast iron pan.

Before Anna could answer, Eli walked in the back door. "Anna, there was a message for you on the answering machine. Neal Buckhannon called to say they are allowing him to bring his wife home and wanted to know if you would be free to come and help him care for her. You are to call him back at this number."

Anna took the slip of paper from Eli's hand and replied, "This is not good."

Rebecca asked, "How so?"

"Neal mentioned that there was nothing the doctors could do, and they were just going to keep her comfortable."

Rebecca shook her head and added a concern, "Tsk, tsk, such a shame. Perhaps you need to help. Besides, it will keep you busy, and remind you the power of love is stronger than fear."

Eli raised his eyebrows questioningly, and Rebecca mouthed, "I'll explain later."

***

Two days later, Anna carried out her small suitcase down the stairs and handed it to the Buckhannons' driver to secure it in the trunk before settling in the backseat. When she returned Neal's phone call, he explained how Margaret wanted to live at home for the last few weeks of her life. While he was grateful for Anna's help, he agonized over her returning without Steven in tow.

Anna wanted to question him about Simon, but knew it wasn't the time or place to satisfy her curiosity about how much he knew about the past she shared with Simon.

The drive to the Buckhannon home left her plenty of time to process what she might do next. While she could continue to work in the yarn shop, it didn't give her pleasure like caring for Steven had. She considered asking Mr. Buckhannon for a reference to apply for another nanny position.

Over the past few days, she had learned to leave her troubles in the quiet moments of God's presence. However, somehow, there was still an emptiness with the memory of Steven's giggle or the way his chin quivered when he didn't get his way.

A change of scenery is exactly what she needed to take the focus off herself and concentrate on helping her dying friend live out the last few weeks of her life.

As she got out of the car, Neal stood on the front porch. His eyes revealed a deep sadness, while a forced smile welcomed her with only a few words of thanks.

Tracy Fredrychowski

CHAPTER 18

S imon pulled Marcus onto his lap and laid his lips on his warm brow. "*Mamm,* are you sure this is normal? Perhaps I should go get Anna. She'll know what to do to bring his fever down."

Naomi laid the back of her hand on her grandson's forehead and chuckled. "Oh, Simon, you worry too much. The lad is just teething. Haven't you noticed the puddles of drool on his chin?"

"But maybe Anna will have an herbal remedy that will help."

The older woman returned to washing dishes and said, "You need to leave the girl alone. All you're doing is muddying the waters by your constant badgering."

Simon stiffened his shoulders. "I'm not pestering her."

"*Nee?* What do you call it then?"

A deafening silence filled the kitchen, and after a few minutes, Naomi added, "Exactly. God will find a way to soften her heart if it's meant to be."

Simon put Marcus in his highchair and pushed his arms into his coat sleeve. "And what if He doesn't?"

"Then you'll move on. But until then, I'm plenty capable of helping you with the child. So, get out of my kitchen and leave us be. Your father needs you more in the barn than I need you in here. I didn't raise all you boys to not know what to do with a teething baby." She shooed him away. "Now, out!"

Simon gave his mother a puzzled glance and headed to the barn. His mind, filled with thoughts of Anna, circled back to the disappointed expression on her face the day he'd picked up Marcus. The need to see her, mixed with a heavy breakfast, stirred in his stomach, making his mouth water.

Going against his mother's advice, he planned to swing around to the Bricker farm on his way to pick up lumber that afternoon. He prayed she'd give him a few minutes of her time.

He picked up a pitchfork with a faraway look and helped his *bruder* lay fresh bedding under the row of dairy cows. The familiar barn bantering did little to pull him from his mission to prove to Anna that he was worthy of her attention.

***

Anna pulled the blanket over Margaret's body and sat down next to her head. "What else can I do for you this morning? Are you up for a cup of tea yet?"

Margaret's weakened state left her little energy to even communicate. Still, Anna knew what the woman wanted most was her company. "Please…ju…just sit with…me."

"I'll sit right here for as long as you want." Anna stood and walked to the window. "How about I open the drapes? The sun is so pretty glistening off the frozen lake."

Margaret barely opened her eyes, but her lips turned slightly upward. Anna sat and asked, "Would you like me to read to you some more?"

"No…tell me ab…about Steven."

A sudden rush of remorse settled in Anna's chest. How could she admit to her friend that she had shut both Steven and Simon out of her life? Instead of answering, she smiled at her friend, hoping some comforting words would come.

Margaret opened her eyes. "Remember the day you told me about your friend?"

Anna tilted her head, trying to recall the conversation.

Margaret uttered, "Mr. Maybe."

"*Jah*."

In the two weeks Anna had been caring for Mrs. Buckhannon, the woman barely had enough strength to formulate a complete sentence, but Margaret took in a ragged breath and said, "I knew your Mr. Maybe was Simon. You coming to care for Steven was an answer to a prayer. God sent you here to fall in love with your future child, and you didn't even know it."

Anna started denying God's plan, but Margaret held up a shaky finger. "The Lord doesn't make mistakes. I've come to learn how much God loves us; even in the middle of our denial and sinful nature, he provides answers to our deepest desires."

Margaret pointed to a glass of water, and Anna helped her take a drink before the woman continued, "That afternoon, it dawned on me that our little boy was enjoying time with his future mother: you just didn't know it yet. I wanted to shout for joy because I had lain here for months agonizing over my inability to care for Cora's child. I prayed God would send us the answer. And he sent you."

Margaret struggled to clear her lungs, and Anna helped her sit up to dislodge a cough before the woman fell back to her pillow. After a few calming breaths, she continued, "It became clear to me that day that I'd be leaving this world soon, and once I realized you were the woman Simon's heart was wrapped around, I was at peace."

Anna asked, "But how did you know that?"

"Oh, Anna. Cora tried everything she could to entice Simon, but he never faltered from his love for you. He didn't even know Steven was his until after he was born. His plans were always to go back to you. Take the money he had made fishing and build you the house and herb farm of your dreams."

A small gasp escaped Anna's lips as she tried to say, "But…I thought…"

"I can see in your face what you thought, but the man loves you. How can you not see that? I had prayed for a woman to take Cora's place, and here you are."

Anna turned her face to the window, and silence reigned. When she returned her glance to Margaret, the woman had closed her eyes and slipped into a deep sleep. Later that evening, Margaret joined Cora by taking her last breath with

Neal knelt beside her, with his words of endearment still heavy on Margaret's lips.

***

One week later to the day, Anna returned to Willow Springs. Pushing a snow drift away from the door with her foot, she stepped into the loving warmth of her *schwester's* kitchen.

The house was quiet, and she wandered into her room, threw herself across the bed, and then despite all reasoning, gave way to tears. She wasn't even sure what she was crying about, but she lay exhausted and quiet. A warm sensation surrounded her, bringing reassurance in place of where sorrow once reigned. "Oh, Jesus, please forgive me for not trusting in your plan," she murmured.

For the next few weeks, she hovered in a silent ache and remorse that hadn't left her since the day she closed the door on Simon.

Each morning, she woke with a prayer of thanksgiving and a plea to God to help her find a way to open her heart back up. Trusting in His ultimate timing, she busied herself and waited.

Spring had arrived early in Northwestern Pennsylvania, and new life could be seen everywhere. The trees were budding, the crocus was making its way through the thawing ground, and Eli's sheep were lambing. As she gathered eggs, her attention was drawn to the buggy making its way up the Bricker driveway. After locking the gate to the hen house, she saw Simon balancing Steven between his legs, pulling up beside her.

Simon looked anxiously at her, then said softly, "I'm taking the boy on his first fishing trip. I figured I'd start him out early." Simon paused and smiled at Steven Marcus's excitement at seeing Anna. "I'm sure he'd enjoy your company. He's...well I'm, hoping you'll come along."

Anna set her egg basket on the ground and walked to Steven's waiting arms. Simon handed the child to her, and she melted her lips against the child's cheek. Just as a barn cat wandered by, Steven kicked and wiggled out of her arms. His chubby little legs carried him away, and she marveled at his newfound freedom.

Left alone with Simon, Anna quietly gazed at Steven. After a brief silence, Simon spoke hesitantly. "What do you think? Can we pull you away from your chores?"

Simon looked straight into Anna's eyes, and she flushed under his steady gaze. Her voice shook, and she dropped her head as her answer surprised her. "*Jah.*"

She dared not look up as Simon stepped out of the buggy, fearing her eyes would reveal the longing in her heart.

Simon was speechless at her reply, and it took a few moments before he said, "I know I don't deserve to see you again. And I came here knowing your answer might have been *nee.*"

Simon puckered his lips and gave a clear whistle, which Steven responded to and followed his call. As they stood watching the child waddle his way back, Simon added, "If we let Him, God will heal what is broken between us."

With her eyes fixed on Steven's confident shuffle, Anna responded with a faltering voice. She recounted how God had given her peace about being still in the waiting and was satisfied in His perfect timing. As she talked, she expressed gratitude to God for shaping the path He had put them on. Simon picked up Steven and pulled Anna in close.

"Anna," he said tenderly.

"*Jah?*"

"The good Lord led us down two completely different paths and gave us both the time to navigate them alonē—but don't you think His will for us is that we go the rest of the way together?"

"Do you truly believe that is what He wants for us?" she bade.

"Oh, Anna, I want that so much, I can't even begin to explain the yearning in my heart for us to be a family." His arm tightened around her waist.

She drew a long breath, then lifted her eyes to meet his. She brushed a wayward curl from Steven Marcus's eye and spoke quietly. "I love you both dearly, and if we can go forward together, it will make me happier than I ever expected."

He smiled at her confession and said, "Then it's a plan. And God willing, we will travel together for the rest of our lives."

With their son wiggling between them, Simon led them to the buggy to pick up where their love had ended so many years earlier. Simon drove them to their favorite fishing spot along Willow Creek with two fishing rods extended out the back side of the buggy, a jar of her famous peanut brittle, and a tackle box full of love. With all confidence that God would lead the way.

EPILOGUE

" *Mamm,* I admit I'm finding my need to come to sit at your gravesite less and less with each passing day. While I will miss our chats, I'm getting stronger in trusting the Lord, which is an accomplishment for me.

Over the past year, I have questioned my faith more than once. You taught us to put our trust in the Lord, but I haven't always done that quickly. It was much easier for me to trust in my own feelings. It was a continual struggle to tell myself that just because I feel a certain way doesn't make it true.

Ever since Ruth gave me your special gift and letter of encouragement, I've struggled to make sense of it all.

Life has been a challenge over the last year, that's for sure and certain. I have had to ask myself on more than one occasion if I was relying on my feelings or fears. I was so consumed with what might happen that I didn't allow myself to love. At times, I didn't feel I deserved God's love, let alone Simon's. The fear of what might happen kept me frozen in anxiety.

Now I'm not saying I still don't struggle with bouts of worry, but now I know where to turn when that little uneasy feeling creeps up. It's incredible how just whispering "*Jesus*" will calm me in those times of turmoil.

You would be so proud of Rebecca's husband, Eli, and Emma's husband, Samuel. They both have become such truth-speaking and faithful followers of Jesus. They, along with Bishop Schrock, have grown the new church to a point where we may have to split into two churches.

Even *Datt* and Wilma joined the New Order Fellowship. That was an answer to so many of our prayers. I'm sure you are smiling down on him and the changes he's made.

Mamm, you touched so many lives those last few weeks of your life, and your memory lives on. And you can rest assured that your grandchildren will continue what you started.

As I think over the last year, I can see how many prayers He has answered. God provided Emma with two little farm hands to replace the one they lost two years ago. Rebecca is with child again and is quickly filling her home with laughter. And

Matthew and Sarah have been a blessing to Sarah's father at the sawmill during his illness.

And then there is how God opened my eyes through my dying friend to show me the path He had planned. In that, I prayed and patiently waited for God to soften my heart to the point that I had no other option than to trust in Him and Simon. And because of His every loving provision, Simon and I will be married in a few short weeks, giving Steven Marcus two loving parents.

Life sure has a way…let me take that back. God has a way of turning a fearful believer into a trusted daughter of the one and only true king. It took a long time to get here, but I can genuinely say, *The Lord is my helper; I will not be afraid."*

Barbara's

Amish Truth Exposed

THE AMISH WOMEN OF
LAWRENCE COUNTY SERIES - BOOK 4

Tracy Fredrychowski

Tracy Fredrychowski

PROLOGUE – BOOK 4
Summer – Willow Springs, Pennsylvania

Living so close to the Willow Springs Fire Department, Barbara Miller often found herself lifting up a prayer whenever the alarm sounded. And it was no different from that fretful day in August, eight months earlier.

After sending her husband John off to cut hay, she busied herself in the basement washing a week's worth of clothes. She'd sent Johnny and Charles to the garden to start picking green beans and didn't hear her father-in-law Andy holler for her over the diesel-powered washing machine.

His gentle hand on her shoulder startled her, and she gasped. Andy's long beard shook as his chin quivered, forcing Barbara to shut off the machine. The boys ran through the bank basement door carrying a toad, eager to show their mother their find.

Barbara pointed to the door. "Get that thing out of here!"

Their long faces waddled to the door as Barbara turned her attention back to Andy. "*Datt*, what is it?"

"It…it's John; he's been in an accident. We've called for the ambulance, but it's taking forever to make it here. I assume they are having trouble getting the volunteers in from the fields today."

The children ran to her side. "Is *Datt* okay? Is he going to die?"

Barbara didn't answer but followed Andy across the yard to the barn he shared with her husband. Her sons were quickly on her heels begging for answers, to which she had none. As soon as they reached the pasture's edge, she stopped the boys and instructed them to stay at the edge of the field with their *doddi*.

Two neighbors knelt beside John; one held pressure on his mangled leg and the other to his head. She dropped to her knees and spent several precious moments at his side until the paramedics arrived.

With no thought of it being the last time she'd be with John, she whispered healing prayers in his ear, encouraging him to stay with her. Within minutes, they had stabilized him enough to carry him through the hay field to the ambulance at the edge of the road. Walking beside him, she didn't let go of his hand and continued to whisper endearing words.

Adrenaline escalated as she had to release her hold and turned to face Andy and the boys. "Where's *Mamm*? I need to go to the hospital; can she keep the boys?"

Their little faces with dirt-stained tears begged to go with her, and she knelt beside them. "You'll need to stay with *Doddi* and *Mommi* for now. I promise I'll send word as soon as I know something."

Barbara looked longingly at Andy, and he reassured her. "Go; we will find a driver and be right behind you."

As Barbara climbed into the back of the ambulance, the technician told her to keep talking to John. Struggling to stabilize him, she noticed the urgency in the man's tone. The sirens couldn't drown out the words of endearment she mouthed near his ear.

She knew her journey would end when they pulled up to the helicopter pad. After she promised to meet him in Pittsburgh, she kissed his forehead. She watched as the helicopter propellers picked up speed.

It was like all the air had been sucked out of her lungs. So much so that she folded her hands over her heart and tried to catch her breath as she watched the form disappear in the clouds. She silently watched and prayed and gave over her husband to the Lord.

***

During the one-and-a-half-hour drive to Pittsburgh Memorial Hospital, she spoke tenderly of John. She tried to shield the boys from the severity of it all.

The driver let John's parents, her, and the boys off at the front door. Johnny grabbed her hand, and Charles leaned into her long skirt. The busyness of the parking lot and the strangeness of their surroundings gave the boys reason to shudder.

Looking over their heads, her eyes sought her mother-in-law. "How about you all go find something to eat, and I'll find out where John is?"

Andy took the boy's hands and led them away as Barbara headed toward the information desk. The woman's face took on an extreme hardness as she told Barbara to sit in the small room to her left.

The cold room and hard chairs gave no comfort, and Barbara wrapped her arms around herself and closed her eyes. An hour ticked by as Barbara played the last five years over in her head. Finally, tears formed with the thought that she may not have the chance to tell John just how much he meant to her.

Stepping in when his older *bruder* decided to give the *Englisch* world a try, John became her best friend. When nothing more than friendship bloomed, she was sure he would walk away and let her mend her broken heart on her own.

But instead, he continued to walk beside her until there was nothing left she could do but become his wife. Surrendering her childhood fantasies of true love, she settled into a comfortable marriage of convenience.

No sooner had Andy and Phyllis found her, and she pulled the boys on her lap, did John's doctor appear.

"John Wagler?"

"*Jah*. I'm John's wife, and these are his parents."

Still sporting the white shoe coverings and matching hat, the doctor spoke kindly and to the point. "Your husband lost a great deal of blood. We couldn't save his leg, and he has a severe head injury. I don't have much hope that he will survive."

Barbara heard Phyllis moan and Andy pulled Johnny and Charles into his lap. The doctor's words still echoed in her head as Barbara followed him down the hall to John's room.

The machines hissed, and the nurse moved from his side as she entered. She laid her hand on the side of his cheek, kissed his forehead, and whispered, "Oh John, you've always been there for me. I'm unsure how the boys or I will survive when you are gone, but please don't hold on for us. God will take care of us. If it's your time, please go be with Jesus. Don't hold on any longer."

As she spoke, he opened his eyes slightly, and she didn't know how long she'd have, but she had that moment. "Thank you for caring for me and showing me more love than I ever showed you. Please forgive me for all the times I took you for granted. But most of all, thank you for giving me Johnny and Charles. I will make sure they always know how much you loved us."

Tears came to his eyes as God gave them a few seconds to heal their hurting hearts. Through ragged breaths, Barbara implored, "It's all right, the boys and I will be okay. Please go home if God's calling you."

He opened his eyes wider, and she knew he heard her; still, she repeated it again. "God's ways are always best, and He will take care of us."

A long steady beep echoed in the room, and the nurse quietly turned it off. When she looked back toward her husband, one lone tear rolled down his cheek and landed on the back of her hand. She placed her lips on his as he slipped into eternity.

When her mother-in-law's moan echoed throughout the room, Barbara stepped aside to let John's parents say their goodbyes.

Johnny and Charles moved to her side, and she knelt to pull them in tight. "Is *Datt* in heaven now?" Johnny asked as bravely as a four-year-old could. Charles landed his thumb in his mouth and crawled into Barbara's lap. "*Jah,*" was all she could muster.

Her heart hurt as Andy's strong hand shook as he stroked John's head. When he pulled Phyllis away, she buried her head in her husband's shoulder, and they walked from the room, taking both boys with them.

Left alone, Barbara moved back to John's side, and a deep, gutted sob escaped her lips. Laying a hand aside John's face, she rested her cheek aside his and cried.

The door opened, and John's older *schwesters* and their husbands started to file in one at a time. They were all there to pay their final respects…all except Joseph.

She walked to the waiting room; Johnny and Charles sat on the floor next to Andy. When no one noticed her arrival, she slipped outside. The sun radiated off the pavement as Barbara darted around cars in the parking lot. Finding relief on a bench under a tree, she sat and buried her face in her hands.

An emptiness like she had never known settled into her soul. What she thought was most likely grief became shame as she played the last five years over in her head. In not much more than a whisper, she asked, "God, is this my punishment? Did you take him from us because I deceived him all these years? Oh, Lord, how will I ever make this up to the boys? This is all my fault. I should have been honest with John. Please forgive me, Lord."

Read more of Barbara's story in the fourth book of

The Amish Women of Lawrence County Series:

Barbara's Amish Truth Exposed

APPENDIX

Anna's Famous Peanut Brittle

Ingredients:

1 cup sugar

1 cup Spanish peanuts

½ cup light corn syrup

1 teaspoon baking soda

Instructions:

- In a large heavy cast iron frying pan combine sugar, add karo syrup, and boil until it starts to turn tan, stirring constantly.

- Add peanuts slowly and turn off heat then add baking soda, stir until foamy.

- Quickly pour onto buttered sheet pan and cool.

- When cool, break into pieces.

WHAT DID YOU THINK?

First of all, thank you for purchasing The Amish Women of Lawrence County – Anna's Amish Fears Revealed. I hope you will enjoy all the books in this series.

You could have picked any number of books to read, but you chose this book, and for that, I am incredibly grateful. I hope it added value and quality to your everyday life. If so, it would be nice to share this book with your friends and family on social media.

If you enjoyed this book and found some benefit in reading it, I'd like to hear from you and hope that you could take some time to post a review on Amazon. Your feedback and support will help me improve my writing craft for future projects.

If you loved visiting Willow Springs, I invite you to sign up for my private email list, where you'll get to explore more of the characters of this Amish Community.

Sign up at https://dl.bookfunnel.com/v9wmnj7kve and download the novella that starts this series, *The Amish Women of Lawrence County*.

GLOSSARY

Pennsylvania Dutch "Deutsch" Words

Ausbund. Amish songbook.

bruder. Brother

datt. Father or dad.

denki. "Thank You."

doddi. Grandfather.

doddi haus. A small house next to the main house.

g'may. Community

jah. "Yes."

kapp. Covering or prayer cap.

kinner. Children.

mamm. Mother or mom.

mommi. Grandmother.

nee. "No."

Ordnung. Order or set of rules the Amish follow.

schwester. Sister.

singeon. Singing/youth gathering.

The Amish are a religious group typically referred to as Pennsylvania Dutch, Pennsylvania Germans, or Pennsylvania

Deutsch. They are descendants of early German immigrants to Pennsylvania, and their beliefs center around living a conservative lifestyle. They arrived between the late 1600s and the early 1800s to escape religious persecutions in Europe. They first settled in Pennsylvania with the promise of religious freedom by William Penn. Most Pennsylvania Dutch still speak a variation of their original German language as well as English.

ABOUT THE AUTHOR

Tracy Fredrychowski lives a life similar to the stories she writes. Striving to simplify her life, she often shares her simple living tips and ideas on her website and blog at https://tracyfredrychowski.com.

Growing up in rural northwestern Pennsylvania, country living was instilled in her from an early age. As a young woman, she was traumatized by the murder of a young Amish woman in her rural Pennsylvania community. She became dedicated to sharing stories of their simple existence. She inspires her readers to live God-centered lives through faith, family, and community. If you want to enjoy more of the Amish of Lawrence County, she invites you to join her on Facebook. There she shares her friend Jim Fisher's Amish photography, recipes, short stories, and an inside look at her favorite Amish community nestled in northwestern Pennsylvania, deep in Amish Country.

Facebook.com/tracyfredrychowskiauthor/

Facebook.com/groups/tracyfredrychowski/

Made in United States
Orlando, FL
26 June 2024

48320237R00203